To Margo,

Nicky Fifth's

Garden State
Adventure

Lisa Willever 2017

by Lisa Funari-Willever

Franklin Mason Press
Columbus, New Jersey

For the Jersey kids who spend many miles on the
New Jersey Turnpike and the Garden State Parkway,
turn off your devices and look outside!

To Captain Cliff, an amazing husband, father, grandfather,
friend, and my father-in-law....LFW

Franklin Mason Press ISBN 978-0-9760469-2-9
Library of Congress Control Number 2004112743
16 15 14 13 12

Printed and Published in the
United States of America

Editorial Staff:
Marcia Jacobs, Brooks Spencer, Linda Funari

www.franklinmasonpress.com
www.nickyfifth.com

Table of Contents

1. The Mouse House Trap   7

2. Flor, Flor, Flor-i-da   17

3. Governor Dad   27

4. Should Have Been Joey Grapes   37

5. Greetings From High Point   47

6. Greetings From Trenton   65

7. Greetings From The Jersey Shore   83

8. Greetings From Tuckerton   102

9. Greetings From Monmouth Park   120

10. Greetings From Camden   138

11. Greetings From North Jersey   150

Nicky Fifth's New Jersey Contest   171

About the Nicky Fifth Foundation   172

Nicky Fifth's Curriculum   173

About The Author   175

NICKY FIFTH'S
PASSPORT

N**P**F

Visit nickyfifth.com.

Download and print your free Nicky
Fifth Passport. Use it when you visit the
real NJ locations that the Nicky Fifth
characters visit.

The Nicky Fifth Series

Book 1
32 Dandelion Court

Book 2
Garden State Adventure

Book 3
For Hire

Book 4
Passport to the Garden State

Book 5
At the Jersey Shore

Book 6
Nicky Fifth's New Jersey

Book 7
Nicky Fifth Says Vote For T-Bone

Book 8
Nicky Fifth Explores New Jersey's Great Outdoors

Book 9
T-Bone Takes a Stand For Public Schools

Book 10
Nicky Fifth Fit

Chapter One

The Mouse House Trap

I hate to admit it, but the truth is, moving to New Jersey from Philadelphia wasn't the worst thing in the world. Of course, I also have to admit that I really enjoyed how much trouble my parents went to, making sure that I was okay with moving to New Jersey. Apparently, I made such a big deal about moving, that my parents still felt guilty. Now, don't get me wrong, it's not like they were going to change their plans because I wanted to stay in Philadelphia, but during the past year, I definitely sensed some guilt.

Unfortunately for my parents, I wasn't the only one who noticed. While they were too small to understand why, even my brother, Timmy, and my sisters Maggie and Emma noticed. I began to think that the only thing better than rich parents had to be guilty parents. And since my parents weren't rich, guilty was working out just fine.

My best friend from the old neighborhood, Joey Grapes, gave me the best advice. "If your parents feel guilty, you've got to squeeze them! Even if you're really happy, every once in a while, look a little sad, especially if you really want something or if you're about to get in trouble."

While it seemed sneaky, Joey Grapes, as usual, knew what he was talking about. He knew so much, he even warned me not to overdo it. One time, when his dad ran over his bike, he ended up with a new bike, a skateboard, and some video games. He was definitely the master.

I decided to only use the guilt for important things. The most important thing, of course, would be getting out of trouble. After that, I would have to be careful not to waste it. Since I wasn't in trouble, *at the moment*, I started to think about something I could squeeze out of my parents.

I was too young to drive, so a car wasn't an option. I always wanted to learn how to snowboard, but summer was around the corner. I thought about it for a while and then it hit me. I wanted to go to Florida. Every year, my parents promised we would go and every year there was another reason why we couldn't, usually a new baby. We spent most of last summer moving and never even took a vacation. We were so busy unpacking, I don't think anyone even noticed.

I logged onto the internet and looked up Orlando. I couldn't believe how many cool things I found. It looked amazing and I decided to print every page. Not being very patient and realizing there were hundreds of pages, I changed my mind.

While I stared at the screen, I remembered that Joey Grapes went to Orlando every summer to visit his grandparents. He went so often that he knew all of the local lingo. He would tell us stories about the Magic Kingdom, Sea World, Epcot even though he called them the mouse house, the big fish, and the globe. Epcot was his favorite part because he said you could visit 20 different countries in one day. That sounded like the kind of bargain my dad wouldn't be able to pass up.

Without thinking, I decided to call a family meeting. I had never done this before, but I had seen them on TV plenty of times. I knew I would have a better shot of going if I showed my parents some brochures and pictures. I called Joey and asked him if he had anything I could use.

"So let me get this straight," Joey Grapes asked. "You wanna talk your parents into taking your family to Florida? That's pretty ambitious for an amateur."

"That's right," I answered, "and the way I see it, it's the least they could do. You know, they did make us move to New Jersey."

"Well, I have a folder full of stuff for all the parks and some pictures. But let me ask you this, how are you gonna ask them?"

"I'll just ask," I confidently answered.

"No, no, no," he started. "That's all wrong. Florida is a big trip. You can't just ask them out of the clear blue sky and expect them to say yes."

"Why not?" I asked. "They made us move to New Jersey."

"Yeah, I know, but it's not like they forgot your birthday."

"So what do you suggest?"

"You'll have to work them really hard. You remind them how much they need a vacation. Leave some pictures around so they'll think it's their idea."

"What if they say no?"

"Look sad and get the little kids to look sad and pitiful, too."

That shouldn't be hard, I thought. I always considered my brother and sisters to be a pretty pitiful bunch, anyway.

"What if they say they want to think about it?"

"That's what you want. Don't expect them to agree right off the bat."

"What if it takes them a week to think?"

"Look pitiful for a week. How do you think I got my dog?" he laughed.

"Alright, my grandfather is coming to our house in a little while. Stick everything in an envelope and get it to him right away. I'll call you later."

As soon as my grandfather's car pulled up, I ran outside to meet him.

"Hey, Pop, you have anything for me?"

"Actually, I do," he said, pulling out the envelope. "Joey said it was very important. What's up?"

"No time to talk," I said, running back to my room. I felt bad not talking to him, but I would explain it to him later.

When we finished eating dinner that night, I told my parents that we should have a meeting.

"What did you do?" my father asked, suspiciously.

"What do you mean?" I asked with my saddest face.

"Did you get in trouble at school today?"

"No."

"Did you break something?"

"No, I didn't break anything."

"Okay, then what do you want?" he asked with one eyebrow raised.

I couldn't believe it. It was like he had radar and he knew I was up to no good. I wanted to call a timeout and talk to Coach Joey Grapes, but I was on my own. I decided that my sad face may not have been sad enough and bit my bottom lip a little harder.

"I just thought that we should have a meeting."

"Honey, let him tell us what's on his mind," my mom said as she scraped the dinner dishes.

"Thanks, mom," I said with my head down.

"Sorry, Nick, go ahead, "my dad said, definitely still suspicious.

"Well, last year was so crazy with moving and everything, I think we forgot to go on a vacation. So I thought that we should plan a vacation for this summer, so we don't forget again."

There it was, I said it and I said it with my saddest face. According to Joey Grapes, this would work. I looked so sad, they'd probably offer to take us to Italy.

"That's what you wanted to talk about?" my dad asked, laughing.

"Well, yeah. I just thought it would be nice to go somewhere cool for a change."

"Hey, what do you mean for a change? We always go on great vacations," my dad insisted. "We've taken you guys to Baltimore, Myrtle Beach, and Lancaster. Plus, the reason we didn't go away last year was because it took months to unpack all of the boxes."

"Actually, we're still not finished unpacking, honey," said my mom.

Thanks, mom.

"I know we go on great vacations, but since Emma is three now, I thought we should go to Orlando before I get too big to enjoy it."

"That's very thoughtful of you," my mom said, sarcastically.

"Well, it's been so busy this year, moving into a new house, going to a new school, and making new friends. I just thought we could all use a vacation."

In one sentence I reminded them how they ripped me from my home, my school, and my friends.

"Listen, Nick, I know we always say that we're going to Florida some day, but I don't know if this is the right time."

"Why not?" I asked, pulling out the envelope.

"What have you got there?" my mom asked, with one eyebrow raised.

"Stuff about Florida."

"Let me see," my mom said as she took the envelope. My parents looked at the pictures and started laughing.

"What's so funny?" I asked.

"Nick, where did you get these pictures?"

"Joey Grapes, why?"

"Well, is there a reason you're showing us pictures of Joey Grapes running around without a diaper?"

"What?" I asked, jumping up to grab the pictures. I couldn't believe it. Every picture was of Joey Grapes when he was two years old. They weren't pictures of the Mouse House, they were pictures of his grandparents' house. There were no pictures of the Big Fish, only pictures of Joey making fish faces. Luckily, in the bottom of the envelope was an Orlando brochure.

"Aha!" I yelled as I pulled out the wrinkled brochure and handed it to my parents.

My parents looked at the brochure for about three seconds and then turned back to me.

"Well, what do you think? Wanna go?"

"Honey, why don't you let us think about it?" my mom said with her *you don't have a chance* smile.

Chapter Two

Flor, Flor, Flor-i-da

After the not-so-successful family meeting, I called Joey Grapes. His mother said he was doing his homework and he would call me back, but I convinced her it was important.

"Hey, Nicky Mouse, what's up?" he asked.

"Very funny," I snapped.

"How'd the meeting go?"

"How'd the meeting go? I'll tell you how it went. My mom thought you looked precious without your diaper and they said they'll think about it."

"Perfect," he said, "except for the diaper part."

"What's so perfect about it? They didn't say yes, they didn't say pack your bags, they said they wanted to think about it."

"Exactly," he answered, as if everything was working out according to the plan. "They didn't say no, did they?"

"Yeah, but they didn't say yes, either."

"Listen, now you have time to work on them. Keep looking sad and get those little kids to help you. It's probably time for a runt meeting."

"A what?" I asked. "You want me to have a meeting with a 3, 5, and 10 year old? Are you out of your mind?"

"Think about it," he explained. "Instead of one kid moping around the house, you can multiply that by four. They won't be able to take it. If I had three younger brothers and sisters I could have owned the arcade by now."

"I'll give it a try, but I know it won't work."

"Remember what they said when the Phillies won the World Series? You gotta believe!"

"Yeah, and remember what my dad always says when we mope around the house? Knock it off or I'll give you something to mope about."

"Trust me," he insisted.

I hung up the phone and tried to figure out a way to get all of the kids to my room. After all of the years trying to get rid of my shadow, I couldn't believe I was actually going to invite him into my room. I went downstairs to survey the situation. If I had to get all of the kids in my room, I'd have to be sneaky. My parents would be suspicious if they found them in my room.

I looked around and saw Emma sitting at the kitchen table, banging on her pretend cash register. My mom was standing by the sink, unloading the dishwasher. I had to think of a way to get Emma upstairs without my mom noticing, so I sat down next to her.

"Hey, Emma, what's up?" I asked in my *talking-to-a-baby* voice.

"I'm the cash regifer lady. You wanna buy somefin?"

"Sure," I said, looking at the play food and lunch bags scattered around the table.

"You gotta pick out foods and gib it to me cause I'm the cash regifer lady."

"Oh, okay," I said picking up a plastic banana. "I'll take this banana."

"That will be sixty hundred forty-two twenty, please," she said, placing the banana in a paper bag.

Not knowing how to pay her, I looked at my mom who was pointing to a baggie filled with pretend money. I grabbed a handful and gave it to her. As she went to open the register, she knocked her sippy cup onto the floor. It must have taken a funny bounce, because as soon as it hit the floor, the lid flew in one direction and grape juice flew in another. So much for spillproof.

"Oh, no!" my mom shrieked as she grabbed a handful of paper towels.

Without hesitating, Emma grabbed a

wooden spatula, held it like a microphone, and yelled, "Cwean up, aisle 6."

I started to laugh until I saw my mom's face.

"Nick, can you do me a huge favor and just play with her somewhere else until I can finish cleaning this kitchen?"

"I guess," I said, not wanting to seem too happy.

"Where we goin'?" she asked.

I didn't answer. I just grabbed her and ran out of the kitchen as fast as I could. The next stop was Maggie, so I took a deep breath and tried to follow the peanut butter smell. I went up to the girls' bedroom and there she was, with all of her rag dolls. She never went anywhere without them and I figured they would be at the meeting, too.

"Hey, Maggie, come down to my room for a minute."

"Why?" she asked.

"Because."

"Because why?"

"Because I said so."

"No," she said, without looking up. "We're busy."

"Busy doing what?" I asked, trying not to lose my patience.

"Playing," she answered.

"Well, come to my room and you can play."

"No."

"Please."

"No."

It was clear that she wasn't budging. I had to find a way to make her leave.

"Okay, you can stay here. I'll just share my lollipops with Emma."

Before I could take two steps, she ran past me. That was good, I thought, two down, one to go. I walked by Timmy's room and poked my head in the door. He was sitting on his bed, tossing a ball.

"Hey, shrimp, come down to my room."

"Really, Nick? Okay, Nick. I'm coming. I'll be right there."

Finally, someone jumped when I called. The girls could learn something from Timmy.

They jumped on my bed and started talking. The only problem was, they weren't talking to each other, they were talking to themselves, but at the same time.

"Sorry, 'bout my juice. Sorry, 'bout my juice," Emma repeated.

"Where's the lollipops? You said you had lollipops. I NEED a lollipop," Maggie demanded.

"Nick, Nick, what's up?"

"Okay, here's the deal," I said as I passed out the lollipops. "Does anybody here want to fly on an airplane and go to Florida? They have princesses and whales."

"Oooh, princesses," Maggie's eyes lit up

while she unwrapped her lollipop.

"How big of a whale?" Timmy inquired.

"I'm drinky," said Emma.

This wasn't going as well as Joey Grapes promised. I suddenly gained a new respect for my mom and any other person brave enough to teach kindergarten. I grabbed the brochure and showed them the pictures. It was like magic. Their eyes were wide open and, more importantly, their mouths were closed.

"Wanna go," Emma sang, "wanna go, wanna go!"

"This is awesome," Timmy said, grabbing the brochure for himself.

"I'll get my jacket," Maggie said, running out of my room.

"Hold on," I yelled. "I don't know if mom and dad want to go and that's really really sad. So, we'll have to beg them and keep telling them we want to go to Florida, everyday."

"Wanna go, wanna go," Emma shouted louder.

"Perfect, Emma!"

"What else should we do, Nick? Do you want me to make posters?"

This was too easy. This is what it must feel like to be the president or a principal.

"Sure, make posters, make cards, write them letters if you want."

"But I can't write words by myself," Maggie moaned.

"That's okay," I said, bending down to squeeze her nose, "you can draw pretty, pretty pictures."

Emma would be the toughest to train, so I decided to do what I do best and teach her different words to a song she knew. Since she always loves when I change the words to Row, Row, Row Your Boat, I decided to use that song again. I thought of some new words and began teaching her our new theme song:

Flor, flor, flor-id-a, I wish that I could go, to see a princess and the mouse and the big fish show.

While it wasn't Beethoven, it did only take her 10 minutes to learn. Now, it was time to just sit back and relax. I was like an army general and my little soldiers were out doing all of the work. Between the posters, the pictures, and the song, not to mention the sad faces, my parents would have to say yes. As Joey Grapes always said, "*it was in the bag.*"

Chapter Three

Governor Dad

For the next week, the troops did a good job. While I had to push them from time to time, it seemed like everything would fall right into place. Timmy drew posters of airplanes and whales and hung them on the refrigerator, the bathroom mirror, and the steering wheel of the van. Maggie drew pictures of princesses and our family wearing dwarf costumes, or at least that's what she said they were. Emma was probably the most effective. She sang her little heart out, all day, everyday. Of course, there were a few times where she was a bit lazy and I had to be more creative to get her to sing.

I didn't know how much more my parents could take, because I didn't know how much more I could take. I e-mailed Joey Grapes every night and he assured me that things were going according to plan.

One week after the family meeting, my parents called us all into the family room. I didn't know why, but I was hoping they were about to give us the good news.

"Listen, guys," my dad said. "We get the picture, actually all 87 of the pictures. Mom and I know what you're up to."

"What do you mean," I asked.

"Nick, we know that you put your brother and sisters up to the posters and the pictures."

"And that song," my mom said, rubbing her head, "that stupid song."

"I don't know what you're talking about."

"Knock it off, Nick," said my dad. "We saw you hanging Emma's rabbit over the garbage can to make her sing."

"Nicky, honey," my mom began, "we know that you guys want to go to Florida, but this is just not a good year."

"Why not?" I asked with my saddest face. I was biting my lip so hard that I could feel drops of blood trickling down my chin.

"For a lot of reasons," my mom said, handing me a tissue for the blood. "We would love to take you to Florida and we will. It just won't be this year."

"But I want to see the princesses," Maggie cried.

"And I want to see the whales," Timmy pleaded.

"I'm drinky," said Emma, holding her sippy cup upside down to let us know it was empty.

"I know, I know," my dad said. "Maybe next year. We'll see."

That was it? After all of our hard work and the fact that we were robbed out of a vacation last year, his final answer was we'll see about next year. What possible reason could they have had?

"Why can't we just go?" I demanded. "You've been promising a trip to Florida for 5 years now. Why can't we go this year?"

"Well, it's like this," my mom started.

"When we moved last summer, we didn't have the time and because things cost more when you have a bigger house, now we don't really have the extra money."

"How can we not have enough money? You both work and we still cut coupons."

"Nick, we have a big family," my dad insisted. "Things cost a lot of money and we just don't have enough money to fly six people to Florida for a week. We will do everything we can to make sure we get down there next year."

"So, now what, another year without a vacation?" I asked, rolling my eyes.

"Not necessarily," he said.

"So we're driving to Florida?" Timmy asked.

"Well, we're going on vacation, we're just not going to Florida," my mom said with a big smile.

I was afraid to ask. What kind of great vacation could we possibly take without a lot of money? We'd probably just end up doing what we do every Sunday, taking rides out to the country and mooing at the cows. Big deal, I thought.

"Your father and I talked about it all week and we think we came up with a pretty good idea."

Oh, no.

"Since we just moved to New Jersey, and we've been so busy with work and school, we thought we should spend our first summer vacation in New Jersey."

"What?" I gulped. "First, you want us to move to New Jersey and then you want us to vacation here? What's next, is dad gonna run for Governor?"

"Very funny," my father said. "But think about it. We haven't really had a lot of time to explore New Jersey."

"Wait, didn't Christopher Columbus and the Pilgrims do that so kids wouldn't have to waste their vacations here?"

"Believe it or not, there's a lot we can learn about our new home state," he said.

"Are you kidding? Is there a hidden camera here? Are you making a tape for the funny home video show and paying for Florida with the prize money?"

"No, we're serious. While you kids were busy making posters and pictures, your mom and I were busy making a list of really fun New Jersey things."

"That must have taken you about four minutes," I said, in my most sarcastic voice.

"Ha ha," said my mom, "you'd be surprised how many great things are in New Jersey. They have beaches and mountains."

"Wonderful," I moaned. "I wish I never mentioned the word vacation."

"Actually," my dad laughed at the irony, "if you didn't bring it up, there's a chance we would have forgotten to plan another vacation. So when you think about it, we can thank you for bringing it to our attention."

I couldn't believe it. Everything happened so fast, it was hard to pinpoint just where things went wrong. In my opinion, there was really only one person to blame and that person was Joey Grapes. When it looked like things couldn't get any more ridiculous, they did.

"How long does it take to fly to New Jersey?" asked Timmy.

I rolled my eyes. Only my brother would want to know how long it takes to fly to New Jersey from New Jersey, a state the size of a postage stamp.

"Honey, we won't be flying. We'll be driving. We've decided to do day trips."

"We can still stay in a hotel, right?" he asked, oblivious to the fact that a day trip takes one day.

"Actually, day trips are great because we'll always be back on the same day. We won't have to stay in a hotel," my mom explained.

"So you mean to tell me that our fabulous summer vacation will be day tripping it through New Jersey? What are we gonna drive up and down the turnpike and pitch a tent in some farmer's corn field, living off the corn and tomatoes?"

"Well, we'll definitely be on the turnpike, but we'll wait until Emma's out potty-trained before we pitch a tent in a corn field," my dad laughed.

My dad obviously thought he was funny, but

I thought it was the worst idea I had ever heard. Living in New Jersey was one thing, but actually spending a vacation here was crazy. Twenty minutes ago, I thought I'd be spending a week in sunny Florida, visiting 20 countries in one day, riding roller coasters, and swimming in the big hotel pool. Now, the only thing I had to look forward to was spending day after stinking day in our van, driving through the most boring state in the country. Despite our obvious disappointment, my parents continued talking about some old barracks and other equally boring places.

"Okay, we thought you guys might be a little disappointed so we made something to help you understand."

As my mom spoke, my dad opened up something that looked like a science fair exhibit. They must have printed out some pictures and pasted them to the board. It was the scariest thing I had ever seen.

"Come on over and take a look," my dad motioned.

No one moved.

"Really, come on over."

I didn't want to look at the New Jersey exhibit. I wanted to pretend that this was a bad dream, but it was like a train wreck. I didn't want to look, but I couldn't help myself. I slowly walked up to the coffee table and was shocked at how much work they put into their geography project.

"Look, Nicky," my mom pointed to the title. It read Adventures in the Garden State.

I created two monsters. The whole time my tiny army was drawing pictures of Florida, they were doing New Jersey arts and crafts.

"I don't get it," I said, scratching my head.

"Oh, it's easy," said my dad. "We decided not to take a vacation like we usually do. Instead, we'll do it different this year. Since your mom is off all summer anyway, we don't have to go away for one straight week. Instead, we can do day trips."

I looked at this enormous, homemade brochure with pictures of George Washington, race horses, and the Statue of Liberty. It looked like a third grade art project. They even used glitter!

"So, let me get this straight, no airplanes, no hotels, and no Florida?" I asked.

"Sorry, kiddo. But trust me, we'll have a great time. You know what the commercial says, New Jersey and You, Perfect Together."

Well, that was that. My vacation had been reduced to day tripping through New Jersey and my parents were ready to earn an arts and crafts badge. I didn't know how everything got so screwed up, but the name Joey Grapes kept coming to mind. I'd have to remember to send him a post-card...*from beautiful New Jersey.*

Chapter Four

Should Have Been Joey Grapes

Spring flew by pretty quickly and I was so wrapped up in baseball, that I forgot all about my impending doom, or as my parents liked to call it, our summer vacation. Every once in a while they would mention another idea and I did what I do best, by letting it go in one ear and right out the other. That is, until my dad called another family meeting in mid-May. My friend T-Bone was over and I wanted to get him out before he heard about our rotten vacation plans. It was embarrassing enough to vacation in New Jersey. There was no need to advertise it. Unfortunately, my mom told him he could stay.

"Okay, guys," my dad began, "your mom and I have become quite the experts on New Jersey and we found some great places to visit. I guarantee you will all have fun!"

"Is it a money-back guarantee?" I asked under my breath. They pretended not to hear me.

"We tried to find the best places for each week and we tried to combine as many places as possible. So some days we may be visiting three or four places."

"Excellent!" Timmy blurted out. I shot him a look before the word was even out of his mouth. "Sorry," he mumbled with his head down.

"Anyway," my mom said, "we wanted to surprise you, but we're so excited that we decided to give you the details of our first New Jersey day trip."

Before they went any further and really embarrassed me in front of my friend, I stood up. "Actually, I think I'd rather be surprised."

"Sit down," said my dad.

"Alrighty, then," I mumbled while I rolled my eyes.

"Now, school is finished in the third week of June, so we'll use seven weeks to really get to know all of the great things New Jersey has to offer."

"We could probably get it done in seven hours," I said in a loud whisper. Again, they pretended not to hear me.

"Luckily, we picked up some brochures from the Department of Travel and Tourism and there are even coupons we can use, if we plan carefully."

My face was growing redder by the minute. I couldn't believe they were talking about coupons in front of my friend. Why didn't they just hire an airplane to skywrite 'WE'RE CHEAP' over the neighborhood? Probably because they didn't have a coupon.

"So, for the first day trip, we're re going to, drum roll, please, High Point. It's the highest point in New Jersey!"

"That's a very clever name," I muttered. "I'm sure the Rocky Mountains are really jealous."

"Hey, that's a great place. I've gone there."

My eyes popped wide open and my head spun around. It couldn't be, but it was; my good friend, T-Bone, was selling me out. He was smiling and actually encouraging my parents. I should have made him leave.

"Have you really been there, Tommy?" my mom gushed. "Is it nice? Did you have fun? Have you ever been to a place called Sunrise Mountain?"

"Yeah, once. It's pretty cool," he answered.

"See," gloated my dad, pointing at T-Bone. "He thought it was cool."

"Do they have princesses?" Maggie asked.

"I don't think so," T-Bone answered. "But there's a Fire Museum on the way."

"Isn't your mother calling you?" I asked him.

"No," he answered, afraid to look at me.

"On our first trip," my father continued, "We'll go to Newton and visit the Fire Museum, then we'll visit Branchville and have a picnic at Stokes State Forest. Finally, we'll go to the highest point in New Jersey."

I looked at my dad's face and could not

believe he was so excited. Then again, I couldn't believe T-Bone was so excited either.

"What other trips are we taking?" Timmy asked.

"Well, your father and I thought that instead of telling you about every trip right now, every Sunday we'll announce the trip for that week. This way it'll be a surprise!"

They had to be kidding. There had to be a video camera hidden somewhere. A surprise was usually good and this was not good, not good at all.

"Are we finished?" I asked.

"Actually, no," my dad said slowly, looking at my mom. "Stay here for a second so I can talk to your mother about something."

While my parents talked in private, I looked at Timmy, Maggie, and T-Bone. My parents seemed to have lost their minds and, except for Emma, who only worries about having enough juice in her sippy cup, they were all traitors. While we waited, I realized I wasn't even curious about what they were discussing. I was terrified. At this rate, I couldn't even imagine what they were

41

dreaming up. Before I could guess, they returned with their big, goofy smiles.

"Your mom and I just talked about it and we think we have a great idea."

"Yeah!" Emma yelled.

And it was official. They were all traitors, *even baby Emma.*

"This news is really for Nicky," my mom said looking at me. "Daddy and I thought that you might enjoy yourself more if you had a friend on our trips, and since the van seats seven..."

Her voice trailed off and she smiled at T-Bone and then me. I guess she wanted me to jump up and down, but the complete and utter humiliation kept me in my chair. I just stared back.

"What your mother is trying to say is that we thought you might want to invite Tommy on our day trips. What do you think?"

What did I think? Were they serious? Now they want to know what I think. For a week I've broken every child labor law to let them know what I think and they didn't care. Now, they wanted my opinion.

"I think I hate the whole idea and I think my friend does not want to be stuck in our goofy van, driving all over New Jersey."

"I'll go," T-Bone said without hesitation.

Slowly, I turned my head and tried to make eye contact with him, but he refused to look at me. He stared straight ahead.

"Wonderful," my mom said. "Tommy, we'd be happy to have you and I think you'll probably make a great tour guide."

"Hey, that's right," my dad laughed. "It'll be like going on safari and hiring a native guide to take you around."

Yeah, that's exactly what bringing T-Bone on our trips would be like. The only problem was that T-Bone still got lost in our development.

By the time school got out in June, the only thing my parents ever talked about were the stupid day trips. It was like New Jerseypalooza. At dinner, in the car, giving Emma a bath, it didn't matter. No matter what the conversation was about, it always came back to the day trips and it always involved more ideas.

Last week, they bought a new digital camera and printer, without a coupon, so that they could make us each a scrapbook. Then my mom decided that Timmy and I should keep a journal because it would be so much fun.The more I thought about it, the more I appreciated not taking a vacation last summer. Even though we unpacked boxes everyday, at least I didn't have to write about it.

It was the night before the Big Day, our first day trip in New Jersey and the elves were all busy. My mom was making lists, my dad was cleaning out the van, and the kids were picking things for the Day Trip Bag, another of their great ideas. Since we would be stuck in the car for hours at a time, each kid got to pick out a book, a quiet game, and a video tape. I decided to call my grandfather, instead.

"Hi, Pop, what's up?"

"Hey, kiddo," he said, "all ready for the big trip tomorrow?"

"Are you kidding?"

"No, why do you ask?"

"Because the whole thing stinks."

"Nicky, do you remember how much you hated the idea of moving last year?"

"Yeah."

"Well, now look at you. You're happy in New Jersey. You've made new friends, you're on a great baseball team, and you still see me, Gram, and your old friends all of the time. It all worked out, didn't it?"

"What's your point?"

"My point is that sometimes, even though you don't believe it, your parents know what they're doing."

"Pop, they promised we would go to Florida some day and instead, we're going to New Jersey and by the way, we already live in New Jersey."

"It does sound funny when you put it that way," he laughed.

"Except it's not funny."

"Nick, I'm willing to bet that you will, once again, be surprised. Your parents told me some of the places on the list and I know for a fact that you'll have fun."

"Doubt it," I said.

"Do an old man a favor and give it a chance. I mean really give it a chance. Your parents have gone to a lot of trouble and they are so excited."

"So you want me to pretend to be excited?"

"Pretty much," he answered. "Anyway, you're bringing your friend, Tommy, aren't you?"

"That's another thing," I complained, "why should my friend have to suffer?"

"According to your parents, he wants to go with you."

"Yeah, Pop," I said as I hung up, "but if anyone should be forced to sit through day trips, it shouldn't have to be an innocent guy like him."

It should have been Joey Grapes.

Chapter Five

Greetings From High Point

When the morning of the big day arrived, everyone looked really excited. I could barely open my eyes and I didn't understand why we had to leave at 6:00 am.

"Nick, do you have everything you need?" my mom hollered as she walked by my room.

"Yeah."

"Can you grab Emma for me and bring her to the car?"

As I carried Emma, I felt someone knock the baseball hat right off of my head. I turned around and there was T-Bone with is big goofy smile.

"Hey," I said, still annoyed that he was so happy to go on this trip.

"Is your dad around?" he asked. "My dad sent this note with some directions and tips."

"Great," I mumbled.

"Good morning, Tommy," my parents said as they walked toward the van.

"Good morning, Mr.and Mrs. A. Here's a note from my dad."

"Thank you," my mom said as she took the note.

Within three minutes, we were on our way to High Point, New Jersey. I didn't know the exact itinerary, but I also didn't care.

"So what's the plan, Mr. A?"

"Well, Tommy, we're sticking with the original plan and then we have a few surprises."

"Good deal, Mr. A."

"Thanks, Tommy."

My parents were so happy that someone was excited, they didn't even notice that he wasn't a part of the family. We drove for what seemed like days, but was only about 90 minutes. Most of the license plates said New Jersey, but you could have fooled me. There were mountains and really tall trees, and tons of farms. My friends from Philly would have never believed it. Then I remembered the digital camera.

"Hey, mom, do I still have to take pictures?" I said, trying to act like I was doing her a favor.

"I'd really appreciate it," she said as she handed me the digital camera.

We arrived at the Newton Fire Museum. It wasn't the biggest thing in the world, but it was definitely old. They had antique fire trucks, equipment and really old pictures. I didn't mean to be interested in reading the little signs, it just kind of happened. Much to my surprise, even Maggie and Emma seemed to enjoy the old fire trucks and the fake firefighter. When we finished looking around the museum, we walked through the town.

About 20 minutes later, we piled back into the van and headed to Stokes State Forest. I couldn't figure out why we had to drive almost two hours to see trees when there were trees in our neighborhood. As we got closer, I knew why. These trees were gigantic and there had to be millions of them.

"Guys, look out the window and you'll see the Tillman Ravine, it's a 10,000 year old gorge."

"What's a gorge?" asked Timmy.

"It's like a hole in the earth," my mom answered.

"Is 10,000 years a lot?" asked Maggie.

"Sure is," said my dad.

"How old will I be when I'm 10,000?"

"Maggie, people don't live...never mind," my dad stopped, cleverly avoiding a difficult death conversation with a five year old.

"When are we gonna eat?" Timmy asked.

"When we get to Sunrise Mountain, honey."

"Where's that?"

"Well," my mom said and then paused.

"Well, what?" my father asked.

"Well, I'm not sure if we're going the right way."

"Why, dear?" he asked politely for Tommy's benefit.

This was actually funny. They had been planning this trip for three months and never bothered to get a map of the forest. I wanted to laugh out loud but it probably wouldn't have been a great idea. We drove around on stone roads that wound up and down the steep mountain. We passed small lakes and a pretty big lake, and we even passed one lake three times. This was probably the one time my father would have asked for directions, but there was no one to ask.

"I'm hungry," Maggie moaned.

"I'm drinky," said Emma.

"Alright, a few more minutes," said my dad, even though it could have been a few more hours.

Then, from out of no where, we noticed a sign for Sunrise Mountain. Even I had to admit it was pretty cool. It was a clear day, so we could see for miles and miles in every direction. As soon as my dad took a deep breath, he seemed relaxed, forgetting we were lost.

"Dad, who are the people with the big backpacks?" I asked.

"Oh, they're hiking the Appalachian Trail."

"What's that?"

"Well, it's a trail that people can hike up and down the east coast, from Maine to Georgia."

"Do you mean that those people started out in Maine and they're walking to Georgia?"

"Not necessarily. They don't have to hike the whole thing. I'm sure some people do, but these people might only be hiking a part of it, he explained."

I had to laugh to think that someone had actually planned a worse vacation than we did. At least our van was air conditioned. As unbelievable as it was, I could now think of the one thing I would rather not be doing.

"Who wants lunch?" my mom hollered from the big boulder where she was setting up the picnic.

It was like a stampede. Everyone grabbed a sandwich, a drink, and a bag of chips. The sun was shining and eagles were flying over our heads.

"Hey, you guys want to take a little hike while mom cleans up?" my dad asked.

"Might as well," I said. "There's nothing else to do."

My dad led and I followed behind him. T-Bone and Timmy fell back a little because they never stopped talking. Every time I was tempted to join one of their conversations, I would hear the topic and change my mind. The last conversation involved trying to determine if T-Bone's sneakers smelled like burning tires or garbage. After twenty minutes, the jury was still out.

We hiked down a steep trail until we reached a small creek. I didn't mind the actual hiking. I just wished we were a little farther down the trail, like in Georgia, only one state away from Florida.

"See this tree, it's a birch tree," Ranger Dad started, "If you ever get lost, you can break off a branch and start sucking on it. You'll taste the birch, just like in birch beer."

"Get out," T-Bone said.

"Seriously," my dad insisted. "Try some."

My dad tried to hand me a branch, but I passed. When I saw T-Bone and Timmy with branches in their mouths, I decided to give it a shot.

"What do you think?" my dad asked.

"Never get lost," I answered.

When we returned to the picnic boulder, we helped my mom load up the van.

"Next stop, High Point," my father grinned.

The ride to High Point from Sunrise Mountain wasn't far. When we arrived at the guard booth, my father handed the woman $5.00 and she handed us a garbage bag. I guess we looked messy.

"What's that?" Timmy asked.

"A garbage bag," my dad answered.

"We just paid $5.00 for a garbage bag?" I asked. "You should have given her a coupon."

"No," my dad laughed, "the bag is for our garbage."

"Why did they give us a bag? Why can't we just use the garbage cans?"

"There are no garbage cans," my mom said, quietly.

"Why?" Timmy asked.

"Well," my mom tried to whisper, "garbage attracts bears."

"Bears!" Maggie screamed. "I don't like bears. I want to go home, now."

This was funnier than driving through a mountain without a map. This time they had outdone themselves. They actually brought a kid who is terrified of bears and bugs into a state forest. I'd like to see them wiggle their way out of this one.

"No, no, no," laughed my dad, "there aren't any bears. Mommy was just joking."

"Sure, there are," T-Bone corrected my dad.

Unfortunately, the correction was most unwelcome.

"No there aren't," my dad said, giving T-Bone the eye.

"Yes, there are, Mr. A. These mountains are filled with bears. They're everywhere."

"No, they are not," my dad said, slowly. "There-are-no-bears, period."

"Oh, you're trying to trick the little kids," T-Bone said with a wink. "I got ya, Mr. A."

"I'm scared of bears and I want to go home, now! I know you're just tricking me!" Maggie hollered.

As Maggie cried, my mom searched through her pocketbook, pulled out a red lollipop and convinced Maggie that it was a Go-Away-Bear Wand. If she saw a bear, all she had to do was wave it and the bear would disappear. Just when

I couldn't believe that she was still falling for my mom's goofy tricks, T-Bone went and opened his mouth.

"Hey, Mrs. A., you don't happen to have any more of those bear wands, do you?" he asked nervously.

"No, I don't," she said, as she exchanged eye rolls with my dad.

I wished she did have one more left. I would have loved to gotten a picture of T-Bone scaring off a black bear with a red lollipop.

We followed the signs, which was good since we didn't have a High Point map, and reached a parking lot. As opposed to Stokes, which was a state forest, High Point was actually a state park at the highest point in New Jersey. We walked up to the benches and I could tell my mom was nervous about being so high.

"What's the matter?" I asked her. "Are you afraid Maggie or Emma will fall over the side?"

"No," she said with a tired grin. "I'm more worried that Tommy will fall over the side."

Next to the benches were huge binoculars. My dad passed out some change and we all had a chance to see New Jersey, New York, and Pennsylvania. It was cool and I took a lot of pictures, but I also wondered if there was anything else to do.

We returned to the van and drove through the park. After a while, we turned into a parking lot and my dad stopped the car.

"Now, what?" I asked. "Are we on our way to Low Point?"

"Actually, wise guy," said my dad, "we're here."

"Where's here?"

"At the beach," he said, with a big grin.

There was only one problem with his theory and it happened to be the one thing standing between us and the Atlantic Ocean - the entire state of New Jersey.

"Dad, I hate to break it you, but we aren't even close to the ocean."

"Oh, my little knucklehead," he said as he

messed up my hair, "a beach doesn't have to be at the ocean. The beach is almost anywhere the water meets the land."

"So, we have a beach under the kitchen sink?" Timmy asked.

"Actually, the only people that go to ocean beaches are the people who live on the coasts. The rest of the country go to other kinds of beaches, like at lakes."

As we walked from the parking lot, I noticed something I never saw at a beach - grass. I also noticed a playground. There was a big building with food and bathrooms and places to get changed. They even had lifeguards.

"Welcome to Lake Marcia," my mom smiled.

"One problem," I began, "we didn't bring bathing suits or towels."

"Problem solved," my dad said, holding a big bag that was obviously filled with bathing suits and towels.

Everyone got changed and headed toward the lake. The water was a little chilly, but once

T-Bone knocked me down, I got used to it pretty quick. Of course, I returned the favor.

I couldn't believe it, but this beach, with grass and without waves, was actually fun. Of course, my mom and the girls spent more time in the bathroom and on the playground than they did in the water, but dad brought a beach ball and the rest of us played volleyball. After a while, we all plopped on the blankets my mom had set out.

"Man, I could go for a hot dog," T-Bone said.

"Well, instead of eating something quick, your dad and I have a surprise for dinner."

Oh, no, I thought.

"That's right, we'll get dried off and head to the restaurant," said my dad.

"About how long will that be?" T-Bone asked in his most dramatic voice.

"Well, the restaurant is about 45 minutes away. Why do you want to know?"

"Because I always eat dinner at 5:00."

"So," my dad said, sounding a little aggravated.

"Oh, yeah," I said, with a smirk, "T-Bone always eats at 5:00 on the nose. He never eats dinner later than 5:00. It's a rule."

My parents just stared at each other.

"Okay," my dad began. "What happens if you eat at, say 8:00?"

"I don't know. I never tried it."

"Well, I think you'll survive," my dad said, shaking his head.

We all went into the bathhouse and got changed. It felt good to put on dry clothes. Everyone piled into the van and we started driving south on Route 23. While we drove, my dad turned on the radio to his favorite station, 101.5 FM to catch the end of his favorite radio show, *The Jersey Guys*. I never understood why people turned on a radio if they just wanted to hear people talking. There had to be fifty stations that played music, but we had to listen to Craig and Ray, *The Jersey Guys*, talk and talk and talk.

It took about an hour to get to the restaurant and I noticed my mom kept looking back at T-Bone to see if he was still breathing. It was almost 8:00 and I think she was really worried that he would faint. I saw a sign that said *Welcome to Chester* and we turned into a parking lot.

"Here we are," my dad said as he turned off the engine. "Welcome to Larison's Turkey Farm."

"Do you know that part of this restaurant was built in the 1700's?" my mom asked, even though she knew we didn't know.

"What time is it?" T-Bone interrupted.

My parents pretended they didn't hear him.

"Anyway, we're going to have a complete turkey dinner with all of the fixings. You'll love it."

"But it's June," said T-Bone.

"What's your point?" my dad snapped.

"Isn't turkey dinner for Thanksgiving?"

"Do you mean to tell me that you only eat turkey for Thanksgiving?" my mom asked.

T-Bone nodded.

"Well, then pretend it's November," my dad said as we walked inside.

I laughed when we walked in because the restaurant did smell like Thanksgiving. We sat down and our waitress took our drink order.

"You know, when they first opened, they served 125 people for Thanksgiving and now they serve over 1,800 people," said my mom. "I used to come here when I was a little girl. It's always been one of my favorite restaurants."

"I like it," Timmy said, obviously sucking up.

Maybe it was the hiking, maybe it was the swimming, but whatever it was, something made me really hungry. I was happy that it was one of those all you can eat places and they just kept bringing more food. My mom said you could order the whole dinner or you could order off of the menu, but I couldn't imagine how you could smell the turkey dinner and ever want anything else. By the time we finished our dessert, no one could move. Luckily, they had big white chairs on the lawn outside and we all took a seat while Maggie and Emma rolled up and down the hill.

By the time we got home, it was almost 11:00 and Timmy, Maggie, and Emma were sound asleep. T-Bone planned on sleeping over, even though my dad would probably have been glad to take him home. As we unloaded the car and went inside, T-Bone thanked my parents for taking him and for a moment, they forgot how annoying he could be. Then of course, he said one last thing to remind them.

"By the way, what time is breakfast?"

Chapter Six

Greetings From Trenton

When my parents first came up with the idea to do day trips, I wondered why we couldn't do them all in one week. By the time we returned from High Point, I knew why they were spreading them out. Squeezing so much into one day was exhausting. While it wasn't my dream vacation, High Point wasn't as bad as I imagined and it did have some fun moments. Of course, the best part was that my parents realized T-Bone was, as my grandfather liked to say, "a piece of work". I was happy they invited him on every trip because he provided most of the entertainment and he made me look great.

On Sunday night, my parents prepared to make the big announcement for the next day trip.

As soon as T-Bone walked in the front door, they began talking. I think they wanted to start before he said something to aggravate them.

"Okay, guys, we're ready to tell you about the next trip," my mom said with a big smile. "But, first, who can tell me the capital of New Jersey?"

"Ooh," T-Bone said with his hand raised, "Albany!"

"No, Tommy," my mom said shaking her head, "that's in New York."

"Oh, yeah," T-Bone laughed. "My mistake, I meant to say Princeton."

"Exactly how long have you lived here, Tommy?" my dad asked impatiently.

"My whole life," he said with smile.

"Glad to see my tax dollars at work," quipped my dad.

"Trenton, Trenton, the answer is Trenton," I yelled impatiently.

"Very good," my mom said with a sigh of

relief. "And Trenton is where we're going Tuesday!"

"Cool," Timmy said trying to high five me.

I left him hanging.

"We need to be ready to leave at 7am. Got it?"

"Sure thing, Mrs. A," T-Bone said as he walked to the door. "See you Tuesday."

I had no idea what we would be seeing in Trenton, New Jersey and again, I didn't really care. The only good thing was that it was much closer than High Point.

On Tuesday morning, we loaded up the car and headed north on the New Jersey Turnpike. My father was excited that his EZ Pass came in the mail and he wouldn't have to stop at the tolls. Apparently, New Jersey figured out a way to get toll money while the car was still moving.

As we entered Trenton, I realized that we were in a city. It was completely different than Newton and High Point and reminded me more of Philadelphia. First of all, there weren't any farms, cows, or horses. Secondly, there were tons of houses, apartment buildings, and stores. Third of all, there were even more people. They were in cars, in buses, on bikes, and walking all over. I figured this would help when we got lost.

"So, what's the plan, Mr. A.?"

"First stop is the Old Barracks, Tommy. Have you been there?"

"Been there? I don't even know what you're talking about."

"Great," my dad said. "Then we'll visit William Trent's House, the State Museum and Planetarium, and the State House."

"What time is dinner?" T-Bone asked.

"Between 12:00 and 8:00," my dad said sarcastically.

"Speaking of dinner," I added, "My old teacher, Mrs. Bailey, told me about a restaurant in Trenton that's pretty famous. We should go there."

"Do you know the name?" my mom asked.

"It sounded like Morenzo's. I remember she

said to ask for Sam."

"Then we'll try to find it," my dad said, happy that I was showing a little interest.

We parked on West State Street because my mom said it was close to everything. After we fed the parking meter we walked toward the Old Barracks.

"Isn't this exciting?" my mom squealed.

"I have chills," I answered.

A woman dressed in a long, colonial dress and wearing a bonnet answered the door.

"Good day," she said with a smile. "Have we new recruits for the Continental Army here?"

"Yes, we're all here to sign up," my mom said, really getting into the spirit.

"Um, I don't think my mom will let me join the army," T-Bone whispered.

"Don't worry," my dad grinned, "they'd send you back before dinner."

As we entered, there were two men wearing very old uniforms. They told us the barracks were used during the French and Indian War and then the British soldiers used them until George Washington won the Battle of Trenton. It turned out that the Battle of Trenton was the turning point in the Revolution.

"You mean George Washington really stayed here?" Timmy asked.

"Absolutely, he did," the soldier said as he proceeded to show us how to load and shoot a musket. "Eventually, it became an army hospital."

"It doesn't look like a hospital," T-Bone noticed.

"Don't be surprised if you don't recognize too much when you tour the inside," he told us. "Things were much different and much harder in colonial times. Even without the war, life was very difficult."

He wasn't joking. When we saw the hospital and the instruments they used, it looked like the set of a horror movie. Most of the equipment resembled things you would use in your garden or to cut down trees. The last part of our tour was the gift shop and my mom bought two packages of colonial money. She handed us each some colonial dollars, as a souvenir to remember the day.

Everyone, except Emma, was looking at the old money. Unfortunately, before we could stop T-Bone, he walked back into the gift shop and tried to buy a bow and arrow with the colonial money. Luckily, my five year old sister was there to tell him it wasn't real money.

We left the Old Barracks and headed to the William Trent House. It was a huge brick house with a cool, white tower on the top. It looked like some of the old houses in Philadelphia.

"Who lives here?" Timmy asked.

"Actually, Nicky, you'll be very interested to know about the man who lived here," my mom said.

"Why?" I asked.

"Because William Trent was a wealthy merchant...from Philadelphia."

"You mean the guy who lived here was from Philly and he was rich?"

She nodded her head and smiled.

As we entered the house, it was clear that Mr. Trent was rich. A woman welcomed us into the oldest building in Trenton Township, as it was once known. Even though it was really old, it looked like a cool house to live in. The kitchen was in the basement and that's where our tour started.

"Hey, where's the refrigerator?" T-Bone wondered out loud.

"There were no refrigerators because there was no electricity," the woman answered with a smile.

"Then where did they put their magnets?"

"Excuse me?" the woman asked, smile fading.

"Ignore him," my father said, giving T-Bone the eye.

She showed us the ovens that looked like caves, the water bucket for when the ladies skirts caught on fire, and a straw broom. Because there were no appliances, everything took forever and some servants spent their entire day working in the kitchen and even slept there to keep an eye on the fire.

We went upstairs and saw the parlors and the dining room and then went to the second floor to see the several bedrooms. Of course, one room was missing and I wondered how long it would take T-Bone to notice.

"Hey, where's the bathroom?" he asked.

"There was no indoor plumbing, young man. In colonial days, people used an outhouse or a *necessary chair*."

"I don't even want to know," he said making a face and shaking his head. "Forget I asked."

"Now, you'll notice that instead of a box spring, they had ropes tied up and down and across. When the ropes got loose, they would turn these pins to tighten them up. That's where the expression, 'Goodnight, sleep tight' comes from."

"What about don't let the bedbugs bite?" T-Bone asked.

"Actually, the mattresses were stuffed with straw and bugs do live in straw. So that's where the whole expression came from," the woman answered with a little 'gotcha' in her voice.

"Cool," said Timmy and I had to agree.

We left the Trent House for lunch at Joe's Mill Hill Saloon. The waitress looked scared to see five kids sitting at the table, but we were so exhausted from walking that we hardly moved. Emma fell asleep in her stroller and we just wheeled her right up to the table. Besides being exhausted, we were also starving. For the first time ever, my dad sprung for some appetizers and the food was delicious.

After lunch, we stopped by the State House. After we passed through security we were greeted by a tour guide. My mom asked, because we had five kids, if we could take a short tour and they were all too happy to oblige. We went to the Senate Chambers, the Assembly Chambers and the Governor's Office. There were portraits of past governors, even Woodrow Wilson, who later became President.

When we finished our tour, we walked a little further down West State Street and entered the State Museum. I wasn't too excited about visiting a museum until I found out we were going to the Planetarium. It turns out that the museum and the planetarium were both pretty good. We saw a sky show with the planets and stars and then a laser show. On our way out we saw some exhibits about Native Americans and Dinosaurs.

We walked outside, under the tall trees, and found a bench. Emma was still asleep in her stroller and Maggie had just fallen asleep in hers. It was a good thing I was taking pictures or Emma wouldn't even have proof that she was on the trip. My mom reached under Maggie's stroller and pulled out a small soccer ball. While T-Bone, Timmy, and I played soccer, my mom and dad sat on the bench, laughing and holding hands. They certainly seemed to be enjoying these day trips.

At about 3:30 my dad said we should head over to the restaurant, even though we weren't sure of the right name or address. After 15 minutes of looking, we ended up on Calhoun Street. I could see the Delaware River and Pennsylvania on the other side. This time last year, I probably would have jumped in and tried to swim all the way back to Philly.

"Honey, I think we should ask for directions," my mom nudged my dad.

"I think you're right," he surprisingly agreed, pulling up to a Trenton fire house.

"Cool, Mr. A." T-Bone said as he stared out of the window.

"We're not going in, Tommy. I'm just asking for directions. I'll be right out."

My dad knocked on the door of Engine 1/Ladder 1 and then he disappeared. In a couple of minutes, two Trenton firefighters came to the van and my mom rolled down her window.

"Hi, we hear there are a few junior firefighters here."

"More than a few," my mom laughed."

"You can bring the kids in, if you'd like," said one firefighter.

Before my mom could answer, Timmy was unbuckled and outside of the van.

"Do you have a pole?" he asked.

"Sure," the other firefighter answered. "Want to come in and see it?"

"Can I slide down it?"

"Well, we can't let you slide down, but I can send one of the guys down to show you."

"Cool," Timmy yelled.

The firefighters let us sit in the trucks, told us about playing with matches and reminded us to never hide if our house was on fire. One dressed up in his gear so Emma and Maggie would see that it's just a man inside, while another slid down the pole. Just when things were getting good, my dad called me into the captain's office.

"Nicky, this is Captain Rollins."

"Hi," I said, not sure if I was supposed to shake his hand or bow.

"Your dad says you're looking for a famous restaurant that sounds like Morenzo's?"

"Yes," I said, "my teacher said to ask for Sam.

"Oh, that's easy, you want DeLorenzo's on Hudson Street."

"How did you know?" I asked.

"Please, everyone knows Gary and Sam at DeLorenzo's!" he laughed. "But you better get over there quick, they get crowded early."

The firefighters finished the tour while my dad wrote down the directions. Before we left, Firefighter Ted brought us into the kitchen and opened up a closet filled with candy.

"Help yourself," he said.

"Wow," Timmy gasped, as he dove head first into the closet, filling his hands and his pockets.

We thanked everyone and headed to DeLorenzo's. Luckily, those firefighters know their way around the city and we made it without any problems. There were a few people outside and we hoped the wait wouldn't be too long. When we reached the front door, an elderly gentleman smiled at us.

"You made it just in time," he said. "In about ten minutes there will be a long, long line."

"That long?" my dad asked as he opened the door.

"They come from all over for this tomato pie."

"I thought we were having pizza?" T-Bone asked.

"You don't want pizza, young man. You want tomato pie. There's nothing better than a thin tomato pie like Sam and Gary make. You'll see!"

We walked inside and I noticed that the walls were filled with pictures of celebrities. We grabbed a big table in the middle and a woman came over and asked for our order. My dad ordered two large pies and drinks.

When the tomato pies started to arrive, I could see the relief on T-Bone's face. I knew he was expecting something like an apple pie, but with tomatoes. The tomato pies looked just like pizza, even though the slices weren't cut in triangles. We all had different shaped pieces, but we ate so fast, no one really noticed. My dad said that was their trademark. As I tasted my first piece, I decided to write Mrs. Bailey a thank you letter. This was, by far, the best food I had ever eaten. Everyone must have agreed because we almost finished four large pies. Just as we were getting up, a man came over to our table.

"Hi, I'm Sam. How was everything?" he asked as he shook my dad's hand.

"Out of this world," said my dad.

"Great, I hope we see you again."

"Oh, you will," said my mom. "We just moved here last summer and my son's teacher told him to stop by and ask for you."

"Really," he said with a smile. "What's your teacher's name?"

"Mrs. Bailey," I answered.

"Sue Bailey?"

"I don't know," I said, realizing that I never knew her first name.

He pointed to a picture of Mr. and Mrs. Bailey hanging on the wall.

"Wow," I blurted out. "That's pretty cool to have your picture up in a restaurant."

"Well, any friend of Sue's is a friend of ours, so maybe we should get a picture of your family up there," he suggested and then asked his mother to grab the camera.

He introduced us to his mom, Eileen, while his father, Gary, spun pizza dough in the air. We took a picture, said good-bye, and tried to get through the long line that now wrapped around the building. Maybe I would send Mrs. Bailey flowers, I thought.

"That was a good day, Mr. A.," T-Bone said as he buckled his seat belt.

"Thanks," said my dad, "but it's not over yet."

Oh, no.

"There's one more stop on this trip but I want to surprise you."

As we drove to the surprise we passed the Sovereign Bank Arena. My dad told us that it was the home of the Trenton Titans Hockey Team. The sun was shining and The Jersey Guys were on the radio. My mom and dad were cracking up and before I knew it, I was laughing, too. In a few minutes, we pulled up to a place called Waterfront Park. It looked like a baseball field, but I couldn't imagine my dad springing for seven tickets.

"What are we doing?" I asked.

"Isn't it obvious," my dad laughed. "We're going to see a Trenton Thunder baseball game."

"Uh, isn't that a little expensive?" I asked.

"Actually, it isn't. These games are a great deal."

"Yeah," my mom laughed, "especially since his manager gave him the tickets!"

"So where are we sitting, Mr. A? In a luxury box?" T-Bone asked.

My dad ignored him and led us to the picnic area. Our seats were in the terrace, but he thought it might be better for the little kids if they could move around. The game was great and we saw two home runs. I was really happy because they usually hit home runs when I'm not looking and this time I saw both of them. The Thunder won and Maggie even danced with the mascot, Boomer. I started to wonder if my parents actually knew what they were doing or if the first two day trips were just luck. Then I heard T-Bone ask where the next trip would be and I realized that they must have no idea what they're doing. I mean, *they were the ones who gave T-Bone an open invitation.*

Chapter Seven

Greetings From The Jersey Shore

Even though I had my heart set on Florida, I surprised myself by enjoying our first two day trips. I even got out of writing in my vacation journal by agreeing to take all of the pictures and letting Timmy do all of the writing. I wasn't sure what amazed me more, that Timmy agreed or that he wanted to write in that thing. Then again, I didn't care as long as it wasn't my responsibility.

On Sunday night, the usual routine commenced at exactly 7:00. It began with the door-bell ringing, followed by T-Bone walking in, too impatient to wait for someone to open the door and invite him in, and the drum roll. We sat around the kitchen table, not knowing where our next adventure would be, only that it would be confined to the state of New Jersey.

"Well, gang, we'll get right to the point," my father started, "our next trip will be on Tuesday and we are going to spend the day at Island Beach State Park!"

I wasn't sure if we were going to a beach or a park, so I just stared at them. Apparently, everyone else was confused, too.

"I don't get it," Timmy said.

"We're going to the beach," my mom explained. "You know, blankets on the sand, a big umbrella, buckets and shovels, a cooler with sandwiches and drinks. Come on, guys, the beach!"

"Well, why didn't you say so?" I asked, relieved that this day trip would be something more recognizable.

"So, we'll leave at 8:00 on Tuesday morning, unless you have other plans or your parents need you around the house, Tommy."

"No way, Mr. A., I wouldn't miss it."

"Are you sure, Tommy," my mom added. "I mean, I don't want your mom to think we're just stealing her son away."

"Are you kidding, my mom keeps saying she wants to buy you a car."

"By the time this summer is over, she'll owe us a house," my dad whispered low enough that only my mom and I could hear him.

When I woke up Tuesday morning, it sounded like everyone had been up for hours. I went to the driveway and took a second look. I never saw so much stuff.

"What is all of this?" I asked my dad.

"Ask your mother," he growled.

"Seriously, what's with all of the stuff. We can't possibly bring all of this, can we?"

My dad didn't answer, so I surveyed the situation myself. There were blankets and towels, a huge cooler, four beach chairs, a giant bucket filled with smaller buckets and shovels, two beach balls, a duffle bag with after-the beach-clothes, and two strollers.

"How's it gonna to fit in the van?" I asked.

"Ask your mother," he said, looking more frustrated by the minute.

A few minutes later, T-Bone had arrived, carrying his own towel, chair, and duffle bag. My dad just glanced at him and shook his head. It took about thirty minutes to squeeze everything into the van, but surprisingly, it all fit.

As we pulled up to the guard booth, T-Bone looked confused.

"Where are we?"

"At the beach," my mom answered.

"Where's the boardwalk? Where's the rides and the food and the arcade?"

"Island Beach State Park doesn't have a boardwalk, Tommy."

"I don't get it," he said, still confused.

"It's a beach, Tommy. You know sand and water. You don't need a boardwalk to have fun at the beach," said my dad.

"But what if you have to go to the bathroom?"

"They have a bathhouse where you can go to the bathroom, get a shower, or get some food," my mom explained.

"Do they have an arcade?"

"Why do you need an arcade?" asked my dad. "You have a beautiful day, the ocean, and the sand. It'll do you some good to get away from video games. You kids just don't know how to have fun."

Oh, no, I thought. You never want to get my dad started on his kids nowadays don't know how to have fun speech.

"Honey, he was just asking a question," my mom said, as if she was trying to remind my dad that he wasn't legally one of their kids and he should be nicer.

"You're right, let's just set everything up and have some fun."

It was a beautiful day and the parking lot was packed. We parked really far away and ended up making three trips to get everything out of the van. We looked up and down the beach for an empty spot and finally picked one that was halfway between the sand dunes and the water. One year, in Myrtle Beach, we learned first hand why you should never go too close to the water as the tide washed everything we had away.

"Okay, you boys help me with the blankets and the umbrella," my mom directed.

We spread out the blankets perfectly and secured them with some shoes and the cooler. Just as we were about to sit down, Maggie came running across both blankets, leaving a trail of sand from one end to the other.

"Maggie," my mom gasped. "Look what you did! There's sand all over the blankets."

"But there's sand everywhere," Maggie said, pointing to the beach. For a five year old, she raised a valid point.

"I know," said my mom, "but we don't want sand on the blanket. Got it?"

"Got it," she mumbled, even though she really didn't.

Before we were allowed to do anything, my mom passed out the sunscreen and told us to cover everything that would be exposed to the sun while she covered the girls and Timmy.

"Can we go in the water now?" Timmy begged. "Please, please, please!"

"Sure, let's go," my dad said as he scooped up Maggie.

"Whonever goes in last is a rotten egg!" she yelled.

As soon as T-Bone heard the challenge, even though it was from a 5 year old who says whonever, he threw off his hat and started running toward the water. After about ten steps, he realized just how hot the sand was and he started to scream and dance. When he reached the wet sand, he didn't stop; he just kept running, right into the water. It took about 5 seconds until he realized that the water was still pretty cold. He started to run back to the blanket, but as soon as he ran onto the hot sand, he turned around and dove back in the water.

"Tommy's funny," Maggie laughed.

Even my dad couldn't stop himself from laughing. Knowing it would be hot, we all kind of quick-hopped to the water. When we reached the wet sand, we stopped. Thanks to T-Bone, we knew it would be really cold. Timmy and I were standing in the water, up to our ankles, when T-Bone started calling us.

"Come on, you big babies, the water is great."

"I'm coming," I said, even though I had no intention of moving and still couldn't feel my frozen feet.

Then suddenly, I saw a huge wave heading straight for us. I grabbed Timmy's arm just as we were being knocked off of our feet. The wave knocked us down and we washed up to my dad and Maggie.

"Whonever falls is a rotten egg," Maggie laughed.

"Listen guys, be careful," my dad warned. "This isn't a swimming pool. The ocean has a rip tide and you can get pulled out fast. I want you to stay together and keep an eye on T-Bone."

"Alright," we said as we waded over to T-Bone.

It only took a few minutes to get used to the water and the waves were breaking really nice. The three of us tried to body surf, because we were the only kids without boogie boards. After an hour, I realized it would have been easier to part the ocean.

My dad held Maggie in one spot as they jumped the waves and then there was Emma. My little sister looked a sumo wrestler. She had a big diaper under her bathing suit, a sun hat, sunglasses, a life jacket, and swimmies on her arms.

"Erin, she won't even be able to feel the water with all of that stuff," said my dad.

"I know, I just get so nervous by the water."

"Why don't you take the swimmies off so she can at least put her arms down?"

"Alright," my mom reluctantly agreed.

Once my mom realized that Emma wasn't a big fan of the ocean, she even took off her life jacket. It could have been the temperature of the water or the sound of the waves crashing, but much to my mom's relief, Emma never went in past her toes. She was much more content to sit in the wet sand and dig with her shovel and bucket. It didn't take long until Maggie wandered over to help her.

We were having so much fun that I forgot all about lunch until my mom called us in from the water. She looked in the cooler and gasped. All of the sandwiches were gone.

"Honey," she slowly said to my dad, "I think someone stole our lunches."

"What do you mean?"

"Well, I got up here and the cooler was open and the sandwiches that were right on top are gone."

"Are you sure?" my dad asked.

She didn't answer, but she did give him one of those, what am I stupid looks.

"Whoever it was, they must have been fast," said T-Bone.

"Why do you say that?" my dad asked, suspiciously.

"I came out of the water to get a drink about 10 minutes ago and all of the sandwiches were still there."

Just then, my dad noticed a heartbreaking sight. There were about twenty seagulls eating our beautiful sandwiches right on the sand dunes.

"Let me ask you this," he glared at T-Bone. "When you got your drink, did you close the cooler?"

"I don't know. Why?"

"Never mind," my dad said, shaking his head. "Erin, I'll be right back. I'll go get some sandwiches at the food stand."

My dad came back with a box filled with hot dogs and fries. Luckily, the seagulls took our sandwiches far enough away that they didn't bother our second lunch. When we finished eating, Timmy and I went back into the water. I asked T-Bone if he was coming, but he said my dad told him to hang out by the blanket for a minute. Later, when I went back to check on him, he was buried in the sand up to his neck. It was the happiest my dad looked in a long time.

After a while we all ended up on the blankets. Everyone was either asleep or playing in the sand. At 4:00, my dad said we should start packing up and get showers. I was so tired that I told him I would just get a shower at home.

"We're not going home," he said with a big smile.

Oh, no, I thought.

"Where are we going?" Timmy asked.

"We're going to the boardwalk."

"Really," I asked.

"You didn't think we would visit the Jersey Shore and skip the boardwalk, did you?"

I shrugged my shoulders.

"Alright, you guys go get showers and get changed while your mom and I take care of the girls."

Timmy, T-Bone, and I got showers in the bathhouse while my dad loaded the car and helped my mom rinse the girls off in the outside showers. Once my parents were changed we headed to the Seaside Heights Boardwalk.

"This is awesome," said Timmy, as we walked up the ramp.

One side was filled with pizza places, games, stores, and arcades, the other side was the Atlantic Ocean. Besides the boardwalk, there was the Casino Pier that stretched out over the beach and was loaded with rides.

"Let's go on the rides," Maggie said, pointing to the pier.

"I want to play some games," Timmy said, pointing to a basketball game.

"I'm drinky," Emma said, holding up her always empty sippy cup.

"How about we eat first, then go on some rides, play a couple of games, get ice cream, and walk around?" my dad asked. They all started jumping up and down.

We ate dinner at a place called the Saw Mill. It was cool and it looked like a lumberjack's lodge. My dad ordered two pizzas and we looked at him funny, knowing we almost finished four tomato pies at DeLorenzo's the week before. When the waiter brought over the pizza, I realized my dad must have eaten here before. The pizza was as big as the table. It was enormous and after a hard day of swimming, it melted in my mouth. When we finished eating, my dad bought some ride tickets and we were allowed to pick three rides each. When we finished our three rides, we walked over to the antique carousel.

"But, we're out of tickets," I reminded him.

"This one's on your grandfather."

"What do you mean?" I asked.

"When I told him we were coming down, he gave me money to make sure you each rode on the antique carousel. There's only one other one like it in the state. It's kind of a family tradition."

"Is this same carousel you rode when you were little?" Maggie asked my mom.

"It sure is," my mom smiled.

We all rode the carousel, even my parents. When we finished my dad let us each pick three games to play, but warned us that it's almost impossible to win anything.

"How hard could it be, Mr. A.?" T-Bone asked as he surveyed the balloon and dart game. "A lot of people are walking around with prizes."

"Yeah, but how much did they spend to win those prizes?"

"I think I can win, Mr. A."

"Good luck," my dad said as he passed out the money, winking at my mom.

Timmy went first and he picked the basketball game. In about twenty seconds he had lost all of his money. I decided to go next and I picked the throw-the-football- through-the-obviously-larger-than-the-hole game. It took a minute to lose all of my money. Then there was Tommy, he decided to play the wheel. He watched it go around five times before he picked a spot to rest his dollar.

"Let's see," he mumbled. "I can pick a number or a name."

He scanned all of the names on the wheel, selected HUN, and laughed.

"What's so funny?" my dad asked.

"Nothing, honey," he snickered. "But that is your name isn't it, hun?"

"Very funny," said my dad, "you should be so lucky to have a girl call you honey, wise guy."

"You're right. Sorry, honey," T-Bone laughed.

I tried not to laugh, but I couldn't help it. I always wondered if it bothered my dad that my mom always called him honey. Now, I knew it didn't bother him half as much as T-Bone did.

T-Bone put his money down and the man spun the wheel. It seemed like it was moving in slow motion, but the little clicking sounds slowed down just in time to land on HUN. The game wasn't over, though, because there was a second wheel spinning that would tell us what he had won. As the clicking stopped, we all stood there staring. If the third wheel landed on a star, he would have won the biggest prize they had. The clicking slowed down and I couldn't believe my eyes.

"And we have a big winner," the man in the booth yelled into his microphone. "A brand new flat screen T.V. for the young man. Congratulations!"

"Wow, do you believe it Mr. A? Do you believe it? I can't believe it."

"No, Tommy, I can't believe it, either," sighed my dad.

T-Bone jumped up and down until he realized he had 2 more tokens in his hand.

He took one and placed it on DAD, looked at my father and smiled. The man spun the wheel and, as if T-Bone was making the wheel stop with his eyes, it stopped on DAD.

"This is unbelievable, folks," he yelled into the microphone. "We have another winner!"

We were all speechless. It really seemed impossible, but it happened. This time he won a mountain bike. He started jumping up and down all over the boardwalk, remembered the third coin, and walked back to the stand.

"What are you kidding me, kid?" the old man asked. "Go play another game."

"Where do I pick up the TV and the bike?" my dad asked the man, still in shock.

"We're here until midnight, here's two tickets, come back before you leave."

As my dad thanked the man he was still shaking his head. The man was shaking his head, too.

"You know, Mr. A," said T-Bone, "I think you should have the TV. After all, it was your dollar."

"Really?" my dad asked. "What about the bike?"

"Absolutely not!" my mom interjected, this time giving my dad the eye. "That's your TV and your bike. You won it fair and square and we wouldn't dream of taking them."

"Yeah, I guess you're right," T-Bone said. "But it was your money, so here you go, hun. Here's three dollars back."

"Thanks, a lot" my dad said, shocked that my mom wouldn't let him take the TV or the bike.

We finished out the night with some ice cream and funnel cake and brought home some Salt Water Taffy. When we got home, my dad still looked puzzled. Watching T-Bone win twice, with his money, was more than he could take. He walked in the house and went straight upstairs as my friend hollered, "Goodnight, hun."

Chapter Eight

Greetings From Tuckerton

By the time our next Sunday meeting rolled around, we were very curious about our next day trip. The beach and the boardwalk were so much fun, I was thinking about asking to do it again.

At exactly 7:00, Sunday night, the doorbell rang, T-Bone walked in, and my parents started the meeting.

"Okay, who's ready to hear about the next trip?" asked my dad.

"We are!" shouted Timmy, Maggie, and Emma.

"Good, because our next trip will take us to Tuckerton and Long Beach Island!"

Silence. No one knew what he was talking about.

"What's that?" T-Bone asked.

"Well, my father had a very good friend who lived in Tuckerton, New Jersey. His name was Captain Cliff and he was a fisherman. We used to go down and see him when I was a kid. Unfortunately, he died a few years ago and his wife always tells Grandpop that we should go down and use the boat."

"Is it at the shore?" I asked.

"Well, it's at the shore, but not at the beach."

"I don't get it," said Timmy.

"We're going to the shore, but now you'll get to see a different type of shore. His house is on the lagoon and when you go out back, instead of a yard, they have a deck and a dock."

"When you say a dock, do you mean they have water in their yard?" I asked.

"That's right. Most of the houses are on the lagoon and he has a big boat, a row boat, and a paddle boat that we can use."

"But there's no beach and sand?" Timmy asked.

"No beach and no sand, kiddo. But trust me, it's a lot of fun."

"Is there a boardwalk?"

"Well, no, they don't have a boardwalk either."

"Then what will we do?"

"Plenty," my dad smiled. "We'll go crabbing in the bay, ride the paddleboat in the lagoon, and take the boat to a restaurant for lunch."

"That must be some parking lot, Mr. A," T-Bone laughed.

"Are crabs bugs?" Maggie asked, very seriously.

"No, sweetie, they're not bugs," my dad said, answering her question while ignoring T-Bone.

"Just be here at 7:00 Tuesday morning, Tommy," said my dad. "That is, unless your mom really needs you. Because, if she does, we would completely understand."

"Not a chance. My mom says that Tuesdays are now her favorite day of the week."

"I believe it," my dad mumbled, as he ended the meeting.

When Tuesday morning rolled around, I had mixed feelings about this trip. If we were driving all the way back to the shore, I thought we should at least go the beach and the boardwalk.

I went downstairs to help my dad load the car. Thankfully, we had less stuff than last time and he seemed like he was in a good mood. In fact, he must have been in a great mood, because as soon as T-Bone walked up, he patted him on the head. Luckily, T-Bone didn't call him hun.

The drive to Tuckerton was a little over an hour and as we entered the town, you could see the lagoons behind the houses. I thought it must have been cool to live on the water. Probably like living in Venice. Before we knew it, we had turned onto Bass Road.

We pulled up to a big house with a stone driveway and a lighthouse out front. Next to the lighthouse was a little wooden bridge. My grandfather had given us the key and when we opened the door, there was a note from Captain Cliff's wife.

Hi guys,

Please make yourselves at home. The key to the boat is above the sink. You can get gas at the end of the lagoon. Help yourself to any food and feel free to use the shower. If you have any questions, you can call me at home.

Give my best to your dad.
Patti

The house really looked like a fisherman's house with fishing nets hung all over. I went right to the sliding doors to see the deck and the dock. The deck wrapped around the whole house with steps that led to a small yard. At the end of the yard was the dock with all three boats bobbing in the water.

"Pretty nice, huh?" asked my dad.

"Cool," said Timmy, as we all stepped onto the dock.

"Well, let's not waste time," he said. "Let's go crabbing."

"How do we do that?" asked T-Bone.

"We have to get the bait, the string, and the nets."

"Here's a string," Timmy said, pulling up a string that was in the water.

"No, no, that's a hotel. Leave it alone," warned my dad.

It was too late, Timmy had already pulled it up.

"Hey, look dad, I already caught some crabs," Timmy said, looking very proud of himself.

"No, the hotel trap caught the crabs. We're going to catch the crabs with a piece of fish and a string."

"Why," I asked. "They seem to like checking into this hotel and all we have to do is sit here and empty it."

"Because we're going on the boat and I'm going to teach you how to crab, that's why."

To me, it seemed like washing clothes by hand when there's a washing machine in the next room, but this whole catching crabs with a string seemed pretty important to my dad. We loaded the boat with all of the supplies we would need, most of which turned out to be snacks. I wasn't crazy about the life jacket, but I knew that it wasn't an issue my dad would negotiate. Still, I felt like Emma at the beach. We started out slowly, as we made our way through the lagoon.

"Why don't you give her some gas and see what she's made of, Mr. A?"

"First of all, Tommy, we're only going to get gas and second of all, you're supposed to drive slowly through the lagoon.If you go fast you'll cause a wake."

"A what?" Timmy asked.

"A wake, like waves," my dad said, "you know when the water starts moving and then all of the boats start banging around."

We got the gas and headed out toward the bay. The sun was shining and every boat that passed by waved to us.

"Do you know them, Mr. A?" T-Bone asked after each boat passed.

"No, Tommy, for the tenth time, it's just polite to wave to other boats."

We found a spot by the old Stink House and my dad started teaching us how to crab. He said that the best spots were the Stink House, which used to be an old fish factory and by the rock pile. Once the boat stopped moving, the lesson began.

"First, you tie a bunker to the string and hook on a 2 ounce weight."

"What's a bunker?" I asked.

"It's a small fish you use for bait."

We all tied our bunker to the string and hooked on the weight.

"Next, slowly drop the string into the water."

Before we could stop him, T-Bone dropped his string into the water. Unfortunately, he didn't hold the other end. My dad stopped talking for a minute, remembering that he couldn't really holler at him, and took a deep breath.

"Tommy, why did you drop the string into the water?"

"Because you said to drop it in the water."

"But, how do you plan on pulling the string back up?"

"I don't know, Mr. A., you didn't get to that part yet."

My dad looked like he wanted to scream or throw T-Bone overboard. Instead, he gave him a new string, a new fish, and a new weight.

"As I was saying, you slowly lower the string into the water, while holding onto the other end, and you wait about a minute to slowly pull it up."

"What's supposed to happen?" I asked.

"Well, it's not like fishing, you won't feel the crab on the string, you have to keep checking. If you get a crab on the line, I'll grab the net and scoop him up."

"What if he doesn't let go?" I asked.

"Trust me, once he's in the net, he'll let go because he'll want to get out."

"Do we keep the ones that get in the net?" asked Timmy.

"We only keep them if their shell is longer than four and a half inches across."

"I nominate T-Bone to measure them," I laughed.

"Forget about it," he said.

"This board is marked at 4 and a half inches," my dad said, holding up a red board, "so we'll use it to measure the crabs. If they're smaller, we have to throw them back into the water."

"I don't know, dad," I said, "How do you get them to stay still so you can measure them?"

"There's a special way to grab them from behind, so they don't grab you. And by the way, you do not want them to grab you."

"What are all of those sticks in the water?" T-Bone asked as he pointed toward dozens of wooden poles.

"Clammers mark their clam traps with those stakes."

"Do people steal other people's clams since no one is watching," I asked.

"No, people are pretty respectful down here. It's like a fisherman's code. Captain Cliff told me all about it when I was a kid."

"He sounded like a neat guy," said Timmy.

"He was, Timmy. He definitely was."

As the morning continued, we started catching our first crabs. The first one scared all of us when he jumped out of the net. T-Bone looked like the only thing stopping him from jumping overboard was the fact that there were more crabs in the water.

Once we got the hang of it, my dad helped my mom and the girls. Somehow, Emma caught the most crabs and even the biggest crabs. Unfortunately, T-Bone never caught a crab bigger than four and a half inches. Every crab he caught had to go back into the drink, fisherman lingo for in the water. My dad was even convinced that he was catching the same crab over and over. After a couple of hours, my mom suggested we stop and have lunch.

"I know a great place," my dad said as he started the motor.

"Dad, the house is that way," I said, pointing out the fact that we were not heading back to the lagoon.

"I know," he said with a smirk.

We drove through some more lagoons until we reached a restaurant called Skeeters. It was the first time I ever pulled up to a restaurant in a boat.

"Welcome to the Tuckerton Seaport," my dad said with a big smile.

We walked over to Skeeters and sat down. My dad ordered lunch and we watched boats that were docking and some that were just passing by.

"We should buy a boat," Timmy said.

"Well, have lucky Tommy pick out the winning lottery numbers and we'll talk," my dad laughed.

"Are we gonna crab again?" I asked.

"No, let's check out what they have. I've never been to the seaport and Grandpop told me its really interesting."

Our first stop was the Duck Shacks where people showed us how they carve decoy ducks out of wood. The shacks used to be hunting clubs that stored the hunters' equipment. My dad was really enjoying himself until Timmy, Maggie, and Emma pulled their visors down to their noses and started quacking.

Next, we went to Tucker's Lighthouse. It wasn't the original lighthouse, since that used to be on Tucker's Island which was washed away, but it was a good imitation. Walking along the path to the lighthouse, I noticed that the bricks in the walkway had names on them. As we neared the Bayman's Museum, I saw a brick that read "In Memory of Captain Cliff" and pointed it out to my dad.

"That's pretty good, Nick. How'd you find it?"

"I don't know it just kind of jumped out at me," I proudly answered.

Two seconds later, a seagull did the same thing, landing right on Captain Cliff's brick. He scared me so much that I jumped back. I obviously scared him just as much, because he took off leaving one white feather behind.

We walked through the seaport for another hour, checking out Parson's Clam House, the Sunny Brae Salt Box House, the Sea Captain's House, and the Tuckerton Yacht Club. My mom, of course, lit up when she saw the gift shop. She told my dad that she only bought something little, but I noticed a big bag under Emma's stroller. Lucky for her, I could keep a secret.

Before we went to the boat, we walked over to Stewarts Root Beer, a familiar site. We used to beg my parents to go to Stewarts because we loved having them attach the little tray to the car door. I wondered how we could eat there without a car.

"Hey, dad," I asked sarcastically, "how are they gonna serve us without a car?"

"Gee, I don't know," he said, rolling his eyes, "Maybe we could walk through the door."

"Oh," I mumbled, never realizing that you could actually just go in and order your food.

My dad bought everyone some ice cream, then we headed toward the boat. We went back to Captain Cliff's house so my mom could put the girls down for a nap and boil the water to cook the crabs. While my mom was inside, my dad took the rest of us out on the paddle boat. It sounded like fun, but it was no joke. We weren't even half way back when my legs felt like they would fall off.

"Where's the engine?" T-Bone asked.

"There is no engine," my dad replied.

"What do you mean? What if you got a cramp in your leg?"

"That would be a shame," my dad laughed.

Of course, my dad had the energy to laugh because he wasn't paddling. I wondered if there was some kind of law against kids paddling when a healthy adult was sitting in the boat.

When we finally got back to the house, the girls were sleeping and the crabs were ready. It was the first time I ever ate something that I caught myself and it was good. We sat on the deck, listening to my dad's old fishing stories and laughing. I would have never guessed that my dad had fallen off of so many boats.

When Maggie and Emma woke up from their naps, we packed up the car and straightened up the house. My mom left a note thanking Captain Cliff's wife, Patti, and we locked up.

As we drove down Route 539, we turned right onto Route 72. Like clockwork, my dad turned on the 101.5 and The Jersey Guys. Today, the topic was car insurance. I didn't know anything about it, but I wished my dad would have let me call in. We continued down Route 72 and I was pretty sure that we were heading to the ocean. About 15 minutes later, we were crossing a big bridge onto an island, Long Beach Island.

"Where are we," I asked.

"Long Beach Island," said my dad.

"What do they have here?" Timmy asked.

"Well, this is the kind of beach we went to last week."

"Cool, we're going on a boardwalk?"

"Not exactly. They don't have a boardwalk, but they have a really fun place called Fantasy Island."

"Wasn't that an old television show?" I asked.

"Yes, it was," my mom said, "but this Fantasy Island is like an amusement park with rides and games."

We went on some rides, played some skee-ball and then some other games, we had a snack, and then called it a night. I had to hand it to my parents, either they were pretty good at finding the few fun things to do in New Jersey or I had New Jersey all wrong. When we pulled into our driveway, my dad and I were the only ones awake. I helped him carry the girls in and then we went back to wake up the rest of them. As I nudged T-Bone, he started mumbling, like he was talking in his sleep. At first we couldn't understand him, but when we listened closely, we could hear what he was saying.

"Are you sure he isn't four and a half inches?

Are you sure he isn't four and a half inches? Check
again. Check again."

Chapter Nine

Greetings From Monmouth Park

Summer was flying by and it was hard to believe we only had a few more trips left. During the week we were so busy playing ball, swimming, and hanging out, that our trips were like a day off from being a kid.

This week, for some reason, my parents changed the weekly meeting to Saturday. When Saturday night rolled around, T-Bone came barreling through the door. We were sitting in the family room and my dad was trying to adjust the color on the television.

"Hi, Tommy, we're in the family room," my mom yelled.

"What's up with your television?" he asked.

"Everything looks green," said Timmy.

"Maybe we should go back to Seaside and I could win you a new one," T-Bone laughed.

"That's alright, Tommy," my mom said before my dad could say something he would regret.

My dad stopped working on the television and the meeting began.

"Well, guys we're meeting today because our next trip will be tomorrow," said my mom.

"Really?" I asked. "On a Sunday?"

"That's right. We're going to two really exciting places tomorrow."

"We're going to the boardwalk?" Maggie asked.

"No," my dad laughed. "We're going to Monmouth Park."

No one said anything.

"Monmouth is a race track, with horses and jockeys," my mom explained.

"I hate to bring this up," I said, "but aren't we a little too young to gamble?"

"Of course, you are," my mom laughed, "but Monmouth is a family track and every Sunday is Family Day."

"How did you even hear about it?" I asked.

"Well, your mom was quite the little handi-capper, when she was a little girl."

"She was in a wheel chair?" Maggie asked.

"Oh, no sweetheart," my mom said, "a handicapper is someone who tries to pick which horses will win the races."

"Are you good at it?" I asked.

"She should be good," my father laughed. "She spent most of her childhood at the track."

"What?" I asked.

"Well, I would go with my dad and my

122

grandfather once or twice a week in the summer. Sometimes we would even do double headers from Monmouth to the Meadowlands in one day. No matter what, we always stopped at Jim's Country Diner on the way home. It was a tradition."

"But I thought that race tracks were for old men," T-Bone said.

"I'm not surprised," said my dad.

"Did you really go twice a week?" I asked, still amazed to learn about the cooler aspects of my mom's childhood.

"Actually," my mom said, smiling at my dad, "I was there so much, I knew all of the tellers and some of the jockeys."

"Get out!" I said.

"Honey, go get the wedding album," she told my dad.

My dad left and came back holding their wedding album. They opened up the book and pointed to a woman I had never seen before.

"See this woman? Her name is Barbara and

she's a teller at the track. She watched me grow up and she even came to our wedding."

I couldn't believe it. My mom hung out at the race track, knew jockeys, and even had a teller at her wedding. This was definitely cool.

"So we'll go to church at 9:00 and then leave at 10:30," my dad said.

"Sounds good, Mr. A."

The next day, we went to church and came back home to load the cooler and pick up T-Bone. I think my dad was secretly wishing that there would be a message from T-Bone, saying he couldn't make it. The only message was from one of those annoying telemarketers.

We piled into the van and left for our next adventure. It took about an hour to get there and I knew we must have been near the shore, again, when I smelled the salt air. My dad carried the cooler while my mom and I pushed the girls' strollers. The track was enormous and there were green and white umbrellas everywhere. We picked out a picnic table and started to unpack.

"Clowns, clowns, mommy look at the

clowns!" Maggie clapped.

"Pony!" Emma squealed, pointing to the ponies.

"Alright, there's time for everything," my mom laughed. "Let's eat our lunch first and then we can walk around."

My mom brought hoagies and bags of chips. The cooler was filled with soda and juice bags and when we were done, she even pulled out a tub of cookies. While she cleaned up, my dad went over to place a bet.

"Who are you betting?" I asked.

"I don't know," my dad said as he looked at the program. "Maybe I'll do a couple of exactas."

"What's an exacta?"

"It's when you pick who will come in first and second. I think I might do the 4 and the 5."

I went with my dad to place his bet. When we got back to the picnic area, the race was just about to go off, so we all went up to the rail. It was really exciting. The numbers on the board changed every time a horse moved up or dropped back. It looked like my dad was winning until the last second, when the 7 horse came up from out of no where to finish first.

"Too bad, Mr. A.," T-Bone said.

"Yeah, too bad."

When the race was finished, we walked over to the face painters. They painted little flowers and rainbows on the girls' cheeks. From there, we went to see the clowns. It was the first time Emma didn't cry. She was so busy trying to knock his nose off, she didn't notice the rest of his outfit.

"I'll be back," my dad announced, as he headed inside to place another bet.

"Need some help?" T-Bone asked.

"No, thanks," my dad answered.

While my dad placed his bet, we brought Timmy and the girls over to the ponies. Maggie loved it so much that she cried when I took her off. As we walked back toward our table, the bugle went off to let everyone know the next race would start soon.

"Who'd you bet this time?" I asked my dad as we walked up to the rail.

"Two exactas this time, the 4 and then the 2 or the 3 and then the 5."

As soon as the race started, things didn't go well. The 3 horse forgot to run and just stood by the starting gate. The only hope left was the 4-2 exacta and it looked like he had it all locked up. It was so exciting until the 5 horse beat the 2 and the winning exacta ended up being 4-5.

"Hey, Mr. A., that's kind of funny," T-Bone pointed out. "That's what you bet on the last race."

"Yeah, Tommy, it's hysterical."

After the second race we took the girls to the Bounce House. My mom suggested we go out back to the paddock, where the horses get ready. It was cool to see the jockey's talking and the trainers getting the horses ready. This must have been where my mom hung out when she was a kid.

As the horses paraded around the little circle, T-Bone gave my dad a tip.

"Mr. A., I would go with the 2-7 on this race."

"What?" my dad asked.

"They look like winners, trust me."

On our way back to the picnic area, we all went with my dad to bet. This time however, we went upstairs.

"Why are we going up here to bet?" I asked.

"To see if Barbara is working."

"Barbara, from your wedding?" I asked.

"One and the same," said my mom.

My parents scanned the row of tellers and there she was, the woman from the photo album. My mom stood in line and when they made eye contact, their faces lit up.

"Oh, my goodness," Barbara gasped. "If it isn't little Erin, let me see you!"

"Hi, Barbara!" my mom gushed. "It's been a couple of years, hasn't it?"

"More than that if all five of these are yours!" she laughed. "And where's that wonderful husband of yours? Well, hello sweetie!"

"Hi, Barabra, it's good to see you," my dad blushed.

"Now, I think we need some introductions," said Barbara.

"Absolutely," my mom smiled. "This is our oldest son, Nicky. This little guy is Timmy and these are my girls, Maggie and Emma."

"My Lord, I can't believe it. Last time you were here, Nicky was learning how to walk and you were pregnant with Timmy. You really have a beautiful family, Erin. Absolutely beautiful."

"Thank you, Barbara. How is your family?"

"Well, my oldest is a doctor and my baby is a lawyer."

"Wow, you've got all of the bases covered," my dad laughed.

"So who's the fifth kid?" she wondered.

"Oh, that's Nicky's friend, Tommy."

"Well, it's nice to meet you, too, Tommy," Barbara smiled.

"Do you need to place a bet?"

"Sure," said my mom. "How about a dollar exacta box 2-7, 5-8, and 9-1, a two dollar trifecta, 2-7-8, and five dollars on the 7 to place?"

"That's my girl! She can bet with the best of them!" Barbara laughed. "Now, how about you, handsome?"

"No, thanks, I'm too young to bet," T-Bone answered.

"She was talking to me," my dad told T-Bone as he moved him out of the way. "I'll take a two dollar exacta with the 3-4."

When the race went off, it was very exciting. Even though I was too young to bet, I wanted someone to win. I was secretly pulling for my dad, since he decided not to take T-Bone's advice. Since T-bone picked it, I was actually hoping that anything but 2-7 would come out. As the horses rounded the final turn, things didn't look good. The 2 horse was so far ahead he could have tap danced backwards for the rest of the race and still won. The real race was for second place and it was between the 7 and the 8. Within a few seconds, it was over and the final, official result was 2-7-8. I couldn't believe it, my mom and T-Bone both won, even though T-Bone didn't have a ticket.

"Congratulations, Erin!" Barbara said as we went back to her window to cash in the winning tickets. "Looks like you hit the exacta, and the trifecta!"

"And, the 7 to place," my mom smiled.

She ran both tickets over some kind of sensor and I almost fell over when she announced how much my mom had won, $356.18.

"Honey, look," she yelled, waving the money up and down. First thing tomorrow, I'm getting that new heavy duty mixer!"

Women, I thought.

By the time 3:00 rolled around, we had done the ponies, the face painting, the clowns, the bounce house, and the arcade. Sadly, my father still hadn't won a single race, even though T-Bone had some hot tips. As my father went to place his last bet, T-Bone hollered out some numbers. My dad pretended he couldn't hear and kept walking. When the race went off, I realized that my dad didn't tell us what he bet.

"Hey, who do you have?" I asked.

"I forget," he said as he banged his rolled up program on the rail.

I knew he didn't forget and thought maybe he was being superstitious and didn't want to tell anyone. As the horses made the final turn, my dad was jumping up and down.

"Come on, 4-5, 4-5, 4-5!" he screamed. When the 4 crossed the finish line, followed by the 5, he grabbed T-Bone and picked him up.

"I don't know how you do it, kid!" he said, knocking T-Bone's baseball hat right off of his head.

We went back to Barbara's window to collect my dad's winnings and say good-bye.

"Here you go," my dad said proudly as he handed her the ticket.

"You finally listened to the kid, huh?" she

said with a loud, hard laugh.

Even though my dad only won $36.16, he was thrilled and for the rest of the day, T-Bone was a hero. As we hopped into the van, we figured we probably weren't going home and we were right.

We drove down Route 537 for about 25 minutes when I noticed a sign for Six Flags Great Adventure. I didn't want to get my hopes up, but I was praying he would slow down. As he turned into the entrance, everyone started to cheer. We spent all summer watching the commercials and hearing about our friends' trips, but now it was finally our turn.

"Are we really going to Six Flags?" Timmy asked.

"You got it, kiddo!"

"Isn't it expensive?" I asked.

"Not today, it isn't," my dad said holding up empty soda cans.

"I don't get it."

"If you come after 4:00, the price is cheaper

and if you bring a soda can, you get $10.00 off each ticket. Anyway, it's worth it to see your kids enjoy themselves."

"Especially, when we won at the track," my mom laughed.

We walked into the amusement park and it was amazing. There were so many rides and games, stores and food stands. It was awesome.

"Now, we'll split up for a little while. Your mother can take the girls to Bugs Bunny Land and I'll take you boys on some of the big rides."

"Like roller coasters?" I asked.

"Absolutely," my dad answered.

"I don't know if I like roller coasters," said T-Bone.

"Trust me, you'll love 'em!" said my dad.

"Now, we'll meet at Bugs Bunny Land at 6:00 and get dinner. If anyone gets lost, go to a security guard or just wait right at the fountain. Got it?"

"Got it," we all said together.

On the way to Six Flags, the sky had turned from a beautiful blue to a dark gray. It looked like a big storm was just about to hit and it seemed like more people were leaving than going inside the park. Because it was so overcast, there were hardly any lines. We jumped from roller coaster to roller coaster. T-Bone looked green after the first one and I think my dad enjoyed that more than the ride.

After riding Nitro, Batman, Superman, and the Great American Scream Machine, we met my mom at Bugs Bunny Land. The girls were having a great time. When my mom put them on the mini scrambler, Maggie put her hands in the air like she was on a roller coaster. When the ride started moving, she kept them in the air. The other kids saw her and they started raising their hands, too.

We ate dinner at a place called the Yum Yum Palace and afterward, we all went on the huge ferris wheel. You could see the whole park, all lit up, when you got to the top. After the ferris wheel, we hit the carousel, the parachutes, and the boat flume.

"Who feels like having a snack?" my mom asked.

That money sure was burning a hole in her pocket.

"Are you sure you're going to have enough money left over for your fancy mixer?" I teased.

"Sure, I'll just take the money for my mixer out of your college fund!" she winked, knowing we didn't have a college fund.

"Good one," I said, hoping she was really joking.

After the ice cream we went to see the diving show and the Bugs Bunny Show. After the second show, Maggie and Emma were both sleeping in their strollers and Timmy looked a lot like a zombie. My mom looked like she was sleep-walking as she pushed Emma's stroller right into a stone garbage can.

"Maybe we should head out?" my dad suggested.

"I guess so," she said through a series of

yawns. "The kids are pretty worn out."

Yeah, the kids were pretty worn out.

Chapter Ten

Greetings From Camden

Summer was flying by and it was hard to believe that we only had two trips left. When Sunday arrived, my parents told us that our next trip would be to Camden, New Jersey. I was wondering if they meant the same Camden that sat on the other side of the Ben Franklin Bridge, facing Philadelphia.

"Which Camden?" I asked.

"What do you mean which Camden?" my dad asked. "How many Camdens do you think there are?"

"Then can we go over the bridge, into Philly?"

"No, Nick, we visit Philly all of the time, this is a New Jersey day trip."

"But why go to Camden if we aren't crossing the bridge?" I wondered.

"Maybe to see the New Jersey State Aquarium."

"Oh," I said, feeling like they finally ran out of good trips.

"What's with the long face?" my mom asked.

"I don't know," I mumbled. "Haven't you got anything else to do instead?"

"You'll have plenty to do," my dad said as he walked into the kitchen. "We haven't steered you wrong yet, have we?"

I guess he had a point, but I still didn't have high hopes about this trip. They told T-Bone to be at our house by 7:00 and make sure his mom didn't need him. Of course, T-Bone's mom was delighted that he was out of her hair one day a week. It was like she hit the lottery and the prize was weekly trips at Camp Abruzzi.

When Tuesday morning rolled around, I

crawled out of bed. I just didn't have my usual energy. I went downstairs and saw Emma and Maggie wearing matching fish sun dresses and visors. Everyone else seemed so excited.

We piled into the van with only one bag of snacks and diaper gear and two strollers. We're definitely traveling light, I thought. Everyone piled in and I expected to go onto the New Jersey Turnpike, a road I was becoming very familiar with. Instead we drove into a town named Roebling and parked the car.

"What are we doing?" I asked.

"Taking the light rail," my mom said with a smile.

"The what?"

"The light rail," my dad said. "It's a train that connects Trenton and Camden."

"Why aren't we driving?"

"Why do you ask so many questions?" he snapped.

"I don't know," I mumbled.

"Sweetie, we're taking the train because we thought it would be fun," said my mom.

"Sounds like a lot of fun, Mrs. A.," T-Bone said with his big, goofy smile.

We got to the station and stood on the platform while my dad bought the tickets. The train came pretty quick and we were on our way. The little kids seemed to love it and I figured it didn't matter how we got there since it wouldn't be much fun anyway.

Before we knew it, the train pulled into Camden and we started walking toward the Aquarium. I realized that the whole time we lived right across the river we never once went to the aquarium.

As soon as we walked in, I realized, once again, that it wasn't what I expected. Being wrong every week was starting to annoy me. I thought the aquarium would be like an underwater museum, but instead, it was big and bright and everything was alive. My dad grabbed a map and made the mistake of asking what we wanted to see first. At one time, shouts of penguins, fishies, seadragons, and sharks rang out, causing a bit of a scene.

"Okay, just follow me," my dad said, clearly showing better judgment.

Our first stop was the penguins. They were pretty funny and we got to see them above and below the water. There was a 20 foot high glass wall so you could see them play in the water. A young kid was there to answer questions and my mom had plenty.

"Are they birds or are they bird-looking fish?" she asked.

"Actually, that's a common question," he said. "They are birds because of their feathers and front two limbs which have become wings."

"Really?" she said. "Why are they black and white?"

"Well, the black and white is their camouflage. When they swim on their bellies, the black side blends in with the water above them and the white side looks like the light underwater animals see when they look up."

"And they're always ready if they get a last minute invitation to a wedding," T-Bone joked.

"Yeah, they're ready for weddings," the kid said, rolling his eyes.

When we left the penguins, we walked around and came up to the sea dragons. They looked kind of like seahorses and the woman by their tank said they were related. For some reason, they scared Emma, so we kept walking.

Eventually, we came across the tank with the seals. Emma must not have been afraid of seals, because as soon as she walked up to them, she started barking and clapping her hands. Getting into the spirit of things, T-Bone did, too.

"Careful, Tommy," my dad cautioned. "You do that so well, they just may throw you in the tank."

"Really?" he asked.

We all shook our heads.

As we continued to tour the aquarium, we saw hundreds of fish, sharks, and a South American Rain Forrest exhibit with birds. The aquarium was definitely better than I thought it would be.

"Hey, dad, why didn't we ever come here when we lived in Philly?" I asked.

"I don't know. We always meant to drive over," he said.

It was getting close to lunchtime, so my parents brought us over to the River View Café. The windows overlooked the Delaware River and the Philadelphia skyline, I thought about my old house and friends that were still in Philly. Even though it had been a year since we moved, sometimes I forgot that I didn't live there anymore.

"Where are we going, now?" Timmy asked.

"You'll see," answered my dad.

We walked outside and next to the aquarium was the Camden Children's Garden. I had never heard of it, but decided, for once, to reserve judgment until I actually went in. They had a 60 foot sunflower, a dinosaur made out of 4 old cars and gardens everywhere. Maggie and Emma loved every inch of it. There was a Three Little Pigs Garden with the pigs' houses, an Alice In Wonderland Garden, and A Giant's Garden.

"Mommy, can I go in the piggie's house?"

Emma asked.

"No, sweetie, the piggies aren't home," my mom said, trying to move to the next garden.

"Sure they are," said T-Bone. "One went to market, but one stayed home, remember?"

My mom just closed her eyes, took a deep breath, and tried to explain to T-Bone that he was mixing up his pig stories.

"Tommy, the pigs going to market is a little story to help kids count their toes, this garden is about the three little pigs and the big, bad wolf."

"Oh, yeah," he nodded, "and how Little Red Riding Hood went through the woods to visit her grandmother, but ended up breaking the beds and the chairs."

"No," hollered Maggie, "That is not right. It's a different wolf for Red Riding Hood and Goldilocks broke the bears' beds and chairs. Mom, tell him he's wrong."

"Are you sure," he asked my five year old sister.

Maggie turned her head in disgust, looked

at my father and said, "He's not too bright, is he?"

We didn't know where she heard the expression, but were impressed at her appropriate usage.

My parents laughed and I was pretty sure I knew what they were thinking. While we were at the garden, we saw a greenhouse, a carousel and a railroad garden.We also climbed up a huge tree house, something I never did in Philadelphia. Of course, as usual, we ended our visit at Ginkgo's Gift Shop. I was shocked when my mom came out of the store with five t-shirts.

"Do they take coupons?" I asked.

"Don't act like we don't buy you anything," my dad snapped. Then he looked at my mom and whispered, "Did you have a coupon?"

My mom just shook her head. Thanks to T-Bone being on the trip, my mom knew my dad couldn't get mad about how much money she spent.

We left the garden and walked over to the waterfront. Before I knew it, we had reached the U.S.S. New Jersey.

"Are we going on a cruise?" T-Bone asked.

"Actually, Tommy, we're going aboard the most decorated battleship in the US Navy," my dad said.

"I don't know if I'm allowed to join the Navy," T-Bone said as he stared at the enormous ship.

"Tommy, we're just taking a tour."

"Oh, then that's okay," T-Bone said with a sigh of relief.

My dad bought the tickets and we started our tour. The tour guide told us it was 11 stories high, over 887 feet long, and the sailors used to call it the Big J.

"What does the "J" stand for?" asked T-Bone.

Before the tour guide could answer, Timmy yelled, "Jersey! What do you think it stands for?"

We walked through the enormous ship that saw action in World War II, Korea, Vietnam, and the Persian Gulf. We saw the sailors' bunks and lockers, the bridge, and the Admiral's Cabin. As we walked through the ship, it was hard to imagine that some men spent years on this ship and how many sacrifices they made. Learning how important a ship named after New Jersey had become, I felt kind of proud to live in the Garden State.

As we were leaving, an older man heard me say that it must have been hard being stuck on the ship.

"No," the man said. "It was an honor."

"You were really on this ship?" I asked.

"Certainly was," he answered.

"What was it like? Was it hard?"

"It was the hardest and most honorable thing I've ever done. This ship was our home and our work. It was hard being away from our loved ones, but we knew that we were doing a very important job. I also made some lifelong friends on this ship."

"Do you remember where your bunk was?" I asked, kicking myself for not being able to think of a better question.

"I remember every detail," he smiled. "I can even tell you where all of my buddies' bunks were."

"Did you have to make your own bed?" T-Bone asked.

I was relieved that he asked a worse question than I did, even though my dad looked a little embarrassed.

"Son, we had to make our beds and keep everything in order. Part of being a good sailor is being responsible. Can you imagine how messy a ship this size would be if the men were sloppy?" he laughed.

"Do you come here often?" I asked him.

"Lately, I find myself here more often. Seeing this ship, brings back some very fond memories."

"Well, we've taken up enough of your time," my dad said as he shook the man's hand. I think my dad was less worried about the man's time and more worried about T-Bone's next question.

As we walked away, I turned and looked at the old man. I wanted to tell him how cool I thought everything he did was. I wanted to tell him that I hoped I would be as brave as he had been. In that instant, I couldn't find the words or they couldn't find my mouth. Instead, as we made eye contact, I just said, "Thanks for everything."

It must have been enough. He nodded his head and gave me a salute.

Chapter Eleven

Greetings From North Jersey

Our last day trip was quickly approaching. I wasn't quite sure where we would be going, but for once, I was looking forward to it. My parents decided to cancel our Sunday routine and make the last trip a complete surprise. I called T-Bone and told him when to be at our house.

Tuesday morning arrived right on schedule, but unfortunately, T-Bone didn't. I looked up and down the street a few times while my mom contemplated calling his house.

"I hate to call so early," she said to my father. "But what if he overslept? He'd be so disappointed."

"Yeah, that would be terrible," my dad said sarcastically, imagining a T-Bone free day.

We waited until 7:15 and then my mom asked me to call him. The phone rang several times and no one answered. Just when I was about to run over to his house, we heard a car beeping outside. My dad opened the door and I couldn't believe my eyes. Parked in front of our house was a black limousine.

"Maybe he needs directions," my dad said, as he neared the limo. "I'll find out."

As I stood in the doorway, staring at the shiny, black car, the window slowly dropped down.

"Oh, my God," I said with my mouth wide open. "I don't believe it."

"Hey, isn't she great?" T-Bone yelled from the back seat.

My mom ran out to the driveway and stopped in her tracks when she saw T-Bone.

"Nicky, did he steal it?" she asked slowly.

"I don't think so," I said.

"Well, then why is he in the back of a limo?"

"Beats the heck out of me," I shrugged.

"Come on over!" he yelled. "It's ours!"

We joined my dad next to the car. We didn't know what was going on and I think my mom still thought that he stole it.

"Tommy, what is this?" asked my dad.

"It's a limo, Mr. A."

"Tommy, I know what it is. What is it doing here? Did you come by to tell us you had other plans?"

"Don't worry, Mr. A., I would have just called you," he said, holding up the car phone.

"Okay, then why are you riding in a limo?"

"Well, I was listening to the radio Sunday night and they had a contest. If you were the 101st caller and you answered three questions, you won a limo, for a day. You even won the driver.

"Well, of course you'd get the driver," said

my dad. "Never mind, just get to the point, Tommy."

"Oh, you mean the driver. His name is Tony," he said, pointing to the man behind the wheel.

"Hi, Tony," my dad said with a wave.

"Good morning," Tony answered.

"No, Tommy, I meant get to the reason why you're sitting in a limo."

"Oh, yeah," T-Bone laughed. "I was listening to New Jersey 101.5 last night and they had this contest about New Jersey. If you got the first question right, you got lunch for your whole office. Since I don't have an office, I knew I had to get more than one right."

"Keep going," my dad said with a sigh.

"If you got two right, you won a luxury box for one Trenton Titans Hockey game. But three questions was the grand prize."

"What exactly is the grand prize?" my mom asked.

"You get a limo for the day, a bag with $500.00, and dinner at some fancy place in Hoboken."

"And you mean to tell me that you answered all three questions correctly?" my dad asked, still in shock.

"Yeah, it was the funniest thing, Mr. A. I knew all of the answers. The hardest part was remembering the phone number."

"But aren't the last four numbers 1-0-1-5, the name of the radio station?" my mom asked.

"Oh, yeah," T-Bone laughed.

"So what were the questions?" my dad asked.

"Let's see," he said, trying to remember. "Oh, okay, the first was to name the lake at High Point and that was easy. It's Lake Marcia. The second one was about how tall the USS New Jersey is and I remembered that it's 11 stories."

"What was the third question?" I asked.

"Oh, that was the funniest one. In New

Jersey, how long must a blue claw crab be, from point to point, to be legal for catching? And, believe me, I remembered that one. It was 4 and a half inches. That's how I got the limo and the bag of money."

"Surely, they didn't give you a bag of money?" asked my mom.

"Oh, yes they did," he smiled as he held up a bag with a dollar sign on it.

"Maybe he robbed a bank," my mom whispered.

"So, I guess you have other plans, today?" asked my dad.

"Are you kidding? This limo is for our trip today. You don't have to drive, Mr. A. You can just sit back and relax."

"But, Tommy, you should take your family out with the limo," said my mom.

"Oh, no, my parents insisted. My mom took half of the money out of the bag to put into my bank account and she said to give you this note."

My mom opened the note and read it out loud.

Hi guys,

I guess by now Tommy told you about the contest. You've been so kind to include him in all of your family trips, that I felt you deserved to all relax and enjoy your last one. Please use the $250.00, the limo, and the dinner gift certificate to make a memorable trip.

Jeannie Rizzo
PS - And thank you, if it wasn't for your day trips, he wouldn't have been able to answer one of those questions!

"See, Mrs. A., my mom said I can hang out with you guys."

"I don't know, Tommy. Are you positive?" she asked.

"Definitely," he answered. "Are you ready?"

As we piled into the limo, my dad told Tony where we were going. As usual, we headed toward the New Jersey Turnpike. Driving in the limo gave the turnpike a whole different feeling. Even though the other people couldn't see us, I felt important, almost famous.

"I think I want to get one of these when I grow up," T-Bone said.

"Well, knowing you, you'll win one," my dad laughed.

We drove up to Jersey City and followed signs for the Liberty Science Center. It reminded me of the Franklin Institute, back in Philly, because it had an IMAX Theatre. I wasn't a big fan of science in school, but I loved these kinds of places.

As soon as we entered the building we grabbed a schedule of shows. I wanted to go to the IMAX theatre first. I saw a sign on the turnpike that advertised a Deep Sea Volcano show and it sounded cool. There was another one about bugs, but my sisters wouldn't have lasted two minutes watching 55 foot bugs.

My mom and dad let me and T-Bone call the shots that day. After the Volcano show, we went to Touch Alley to test our sense of touch in a 100 foot long, dark tunnel. Of course, T-Bone failed the test when he came out hugging a very scared, very old woman. On the same floor was Perception Alley, which was almost like a fun house. When we reached the environment floor, we could see New York City, the Statue of Liberty and Ellis Island.

"It would be cool to see the statue and Ellis Island," I told my dad, "except that this is a New Jersey trip and they're in New York."

"Well, there's always been a debate about that," he said.

"What do you mean?" I asked.

"Actually, there was a debate about whether Ellis Island belonged to New Jersey or New York. The two states even went to court over it."

"How come?"

"Well, the New York Harbor is between New York and New Jersey and there was some question as to which side the island was on."

"So, which side is it on?"

"Actually, I don't know," my dad sighed. "Let's just say that since it's in the middle of the harbor they share, it doesn't matter. We'll go!"

I felt like a movie star, walking out of the science center and having a limo pull up. I felt like an idiot, however, when a dozen girls came running over to ask for my autograph. Surrounded by fans, I just looked at T-Bone.

"Sorry," he winked. "I didn't mean to tell them about your new television show. It just slipped."

"My what?" I screamed, as three girls were all grabbing my left arm and pulling.

"Just give them your autograph," he hollered from behind the crowd.

I wasn't sure what to do and I couldn't even see my parents, so I signed autographs. To make sure I never got in trouble for it, I signed T-Bone's name. There was one girl who tried to kiss me so I gave her T-Bone's phone number, too.

Not knowing what was going on, my parents came running over to see if I was alright. When I told them what T-Bone had done, they laughed. I was shocked and expected them to be upset. Instead, they both said, "Good one!" Clearly, they were letting T-Bone's limo and bag of money cloud their judgment.

We spent the rest of the day at Ellis Island and the Statue of Liberty. My dad told Timmy how our ancestors came over from Italy with only the clothes on their backs.

"They should have used a suitcase," said T-Bone.

We were all getting tired and just agreed with him. It was easier than trying to explain the conditions of the people who arrived at Ellis Island.

Just taking the ferry to the statue was amazing. When I came face to face with it, I was blown away.

"I hope we gave France a good gift in return," I joked.

"I think we gave them the Eiffel Tower or the Leaning Tower of Pisa," said T-Bone, not realizing that I was joking. Again, we just agreed with him. Sometimes it was just easier.

After the Statue of Liberty and Ellis Island, we went to Hoboken. Never having been there before, I didn't know what to expect.

"Are we at Hobroken, yet?"Maggie asked as she stared out the limo window.

"Almost," said Tony. "Just a few more minutes."

"Hey Tony, do you get 101.5 on the radio?" I

asked. With school coming up, I wasn't sure how many more times I would get to hear *The Jersey Guys*.

"You got it, kid," Tony said as he turned up the volume. He was already listening to them. "These guys crack me up!"

"So, Tony," my dad asked the driver. "Where are we going for dinner?"

"Amanda's on Washington Street."

"Sounds good," smiled my mom.

"I think you'll be pleased, sir," Tony began, "But, there's one thing we have to take care of first."

"What's that," asked my dad.

Before Tony could answer, the phone in the limo rang. No one knew what to do, so we just stared at it. By the fourth ring, Tony suggested that someone answer it. While we frantically tried to decide who should be the one, Emma picked up the receiver.

"Hewwoooo," she said.

Tony flipped a red switch to turn on the speakerphone.

"Well, hello, little dog," the voice on the other end yelled. It sounded really familiar, but I couldn't place it.

"Hey, where's Tommy Rizzo?" asked the voice. "Ray wants to talk to the little Italian kid!"

Oh my God, I thought. I recognize the voice! I recognize the voice! It's *The Jersey Guys* from New Jersey 101.5. I couldn't believe it!

"We've got a whole car full of Italian kids!" my mom laughed.

"Then put them all on!" the voice yelled. "Do you know who this is?"

"Uncle Gordon?" T-Bone yelled.

"Uncle Gordon," the voice laughed, "I've been called a lot of things in my life, but never Uncle Gordon!"

I couldn't take it anymore. We had the actual Jersey Guys on the phone and T-Bone was on the verge of insulting them.

"Hey, dog," I yelled, "you're *The Jersey Guys,* Ray and Craig!"

"That's right, my man," Craig answered. "And we're talking to our New Jersey 101.5 New Jersey Trivia Challenge winner, 12-year-old, Tommy Rizzo, and from what Tony, the limo driver told us, some other kids' family."

"Is that right?" asked Ray, the other *Jersey Guy.* "Tommy, what's the deal with bringing another family?"

"Well, the Abruzzi's took me on a bunch of trips and my mom thought they deserved to go today. She insisted."

"Well, kid, it sounds like you must be some piece of work," Craig laughed. "Let me talk to someone from the Abruzzi family."

"Hi," my mom said.

"Is this the mom," asked Ray.

"Um, yes," my mom answered. "This is Erin Abruzzi."

"So, Erin, what's the real story with this

kid? How did you guys end up in the limo and what did you do with his family?"

"He's really a wonderful boy. We took one New Jersey day trip each week, for seven weeks and we brought Tommy with us. His mom really appreciated it and sent the limo over today."

"What about the bag of money?" asked Ray.

"My parents put half in my bank account and the rest is here, in the limo."

"So let me get this straight, dog," you guys are just driving around, in a limo, with a bag of money?"

"Half a bag, "T-Bone corrected. "Remember, I said that my parents put half of the money in the bank?"

"Yeah, I can see why the Abruzzi's deserved to go!" Craig joked.

"Hey, are we on the radio, right now, because my friend Nicky here is a big fan," said T-Bone. "He's been listening to you all summer."

"Hey, Nicky, Nick! What's up, man?" Craig

shouted. "Of course, you're on the radio!"

"Not much," I answered, wishing I could think of something cool to say.

"Not much?" he laughed. "Do you always drive around in a limo with HALF a bag of money?"

"Well, no," I said. "Just on Tuesdays."

My under-pressure attempt at a joke was successful. For once, everyone laughed.

"So, I want to know this," Ray asked. "We had something like 400 people call in with the wrong answers, how did a 12 year old know the legal length of a blue claw crab?"

"Well," T-Bone answered very thoughtfully, "it took a lot of thinking and I do read a lot."

"Yeah, right," I laughed. "How about the fact that out of the 200 crabs he caught, not one of them was four and a half inches across?"

"Nicky Abruzzi, you are one sarcastic kid," said Craig, "and I like it! When can we have you on the show again?"

"Are you serious?" I asked.

"Why not, they can't fire us for that, can they, Ray?"

"Don't think so," Ray answered.

"Great, you're hired!" said Craig. "Nicky, you remind me of myself when I was very young and very sarcastic. And Tommy, you could be a junior Ray. Maybe you could be our New Jersey correspondents and check out places in New Jersey for us."

"Wow," said T-Bone, "pretty soon we won't be able to walk down the street without people asking us for autographs!"

"You do realize this is a radio show, right?" asked Ray.

"He really is a junior Ray," Craig laughed.

"Hey, is this for real?" I asked, still waiting for a hidden camera to pop out from the front seat.

"Absolutely, call us tomorrow and we'll set things up," said Craig. "Now, get inside Amanda's and enjoy your dinner. It was great to talk to everyone. And thanks for listening to New Jersey 101.5."

We walked into Amanda's and they treated us like royalty. They brought extra things we didn't order and sent round after round of sodas with cherries and orange slices.

On the way home, T-Bone told us that he couldn't sleep over because he had a doctor's appointment in the morning. It was such an amazing day that my dad almost seemed sad to drop him off.

When the limo pulled up to our house, once again, the kids were all asleep. I helped my parents carry them and my mom went straight upstairs to tuck them in. I was too excited to go to sleep so I joined my dad in the family room.

"Pretty exciting day, huh?" he asked.

"Pretty exciting summer," I answered, after giving it some thought.

"Really?"

"Yeah," I said, "it was definitely different than I hoped it would be, but the day trips were actually cool."

"You know, your mom and I were really worried that you would hate them."

"Then why did you guarantee that I'd love them?" I asked.

"Wishful thinking, I guess."

"In the beginning, I really, really wanted to go to Florida. When you told us we were spending our vacation in New Jersey, I thought you and mom were losing it."

"I thought the same thing when I was in your shoes," he laughed.

"What do you mean, when you were in my shoes?"

"One year, when I was growing up, money was really tight and my parents decided to do day trips."

"So, wait a minute," I started. "Is that why you knew to bring bathing suits to Lake Marcia?"

He smiled.

"So you had everything planned so perfectly because you had already been to these places?"

"Well, not everything. No one could have

predicted that Tommy would win a limo and a bag of money!"

"You've got a point," I said, "but do you know how sneaky that is?"

He smiled and nodded.

"Why didn't you just tell us in the beginning?" I asked.

"Your mom and I wanted you to learn that it's really not about the destination. Good vacations are about the people you're with and the memories you make."

"So why didn't you just say so?"

"Well, some things you have to learn for yourself."

"I guess," I said as I skimmed the pictures on my digital camera.

"So, now that you'll be working for the radio station, any idea where your first day trip will be?"

"Yeah," I laughed, "*somewhere in New Jersey!*"

Nicky Fifth's New Jersey Contest

Are You A New Jersey Character?

Submit your favorite New Jersey destination to Nicky Fifth and T-Bone and you could become a character in an upcoming Nicky Fifth book. Write a 3-4 paragraph persuasive essay, selling your idea to Nicky and T-Bone. Make sure your idea is located in New Jersey and hasn't been included in a previous book in the series. Check the website for a list of places already included.

Entries are judged on creativity, writing style, history, and level of persuasion. Do not list numerous locations; focus on one and make sure it is located in New Jersey. To enter your work, visit www.nickyfifth.com and be sure you have your parents' permission.

Prizes:

1st Prize - $200.00 Barnes & Noble Gift Card
> YOUR idea is used in an upcoming book
> YOU become a character in the book

2nd Prize - $100.00 Barnes & Noble Gift Card
> YOUR idea is used in an upcoming book

3rd Prize - $75.00 Barnes & Noble Gift Card
> YOUR idea is used in an upcoming book

NFF

About the Nicky Fifth Foundation

In May 2015, after years of providing tens of thousands of free books to schools and children in need, Lisa Funari-Willever created the Nicky Fifth Foundation to promote literature, education, and awareness for New Jersey children.

With the help of her husband, Todd Willever, and good friend, Iris Hutchinson, the Nicky Fifth Foundation was born. The first step, was to establish a dynamic Board of Directors to guide the foundation. Luckily, Lisa knew many generous, dynamic people.

One by one, all of the board seats were enthusiastically occupied by individuals who really care about New Jersey kids. Along with Lisa, Todd, and Iris, the Board of Directors consists of Paula Agabiti, Karen Funari, Dawn Hiltner, Don Jay Smith, Walker Worthy, Brenda Zanoni, and Nancy Byrne.

Once the board was established, the first program, Nicky Fifth's CODE READ, began.

www.nickyfifth.org

The Nicky Fifth Curriculum

The Nicky Fifth Curriculum brings New Jersey and vital topics currently omitted from test-based curriculums to life. Through humorous, realistic fiction, the Nicky Fifth series allows teachers to present numerous topics to students within the context of literature, eliminating the need for additional instruction time. As opposed to current trends, the Nicky Fifth curriculum encourages teachers to embrace their creativity and adapt lessons to address the needs of their students.

Teachers can seamlessly combine literature with topics such as New Jersey history, geography, civics, government, the environment, the art of debate, education, poverty, and wellness in an age-appropriate manner. Using the familiar Nicky Fifth characters, this unique Jersey-centric curriculum spans grades 2-6, is easy to implement, is inexpensive, and easily lends itself to extension activities. Schools purchase the chapter books and Nicky Fifth provides amazing multi-discipline materials for all learners, at no cost.

Visit **nickyfifth.com** to easily access over 400 printable worksheets, dozens of slide shows, and exciting videos...*all at no cost!* Enjoy!

About the Author,
Lisa Funari Willever

Lisa Funari Willever wanted to be an author since she was in the third grade and often says if there was a Guest Young Author contest when she was a child, she would have submitted a story a day. *Maybe two a day on weekends!*

She has been a wedding-dress-seller, a file clerk, a sock counter *(really)*, a hostess, waitress, teacher, and author. While she loved teaching in Trenton, New Jersey, becoming an author has been one of the most exciting adventures of her life. She is a full-time mom and a *night-time author* who travels all over the world visiting schools. She has been to hundreds of schools in dozens of states, including California, South Dakota, Iowa, South Carolina, North Carolina, Florida, Delaware, Connecticut, New York, Pennsylvania, West Virginia, Ohio, Nevada, Idaho, Utah, Alabama, Louisiana, and even the US Navy base in Sasebo, Japan.

Lisa has written over two dozen books for children and even a book for new teachers. Her critically acclaimed *Chumpkin* was selected as a favorite by First Lady Laura Bush and displayed at the White House, *Everybody Moos At Cows* was featured on the Rosie O'Donnell Show, and *Garden State Adventure* and *32 Dandelion Court* have been on the prestigious New Jersey Battle of the Books List. Some of her titles include *You Can't Walk A Fish, The Easter Chicken, Maximilian The Great, Where Do Snowmen Go?, The Culprit Was A Fly, Miracle on Theodore's Street, A Glove of Their Own, There's A Kid Under My Bed,* and *On Your Mark, Get Set, Teach.* Her Nicky Fifth series has been embraced by New Jersey schools and a unique and innovative Nicky Fifth curriculum has been developed.

Lisa is married to Todd Willever, a Captain in the Trenton Fire Department, and they have three children, Jessica, Patrick, and Timmy.

Lisa was a lifelong resident of Trenton and while she is proud to now reside in beautiful Mansfield Township, she treasures her 34 years in the city. She is a graduate of Trenton State College and loves nothing more than traveling with her family, reading, writing, and finding creative ways to avoid cooking!